44 Hours or Strike!

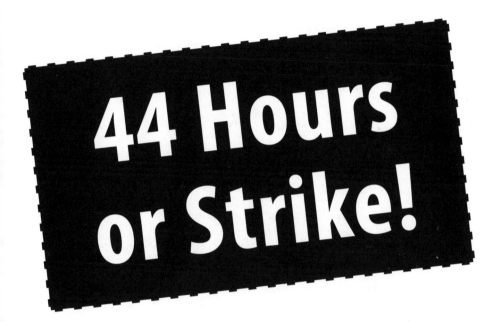

44 Hours or Strike!

ANNE DUBLIN

Second Story Press

Library and Archives Canada Cataloguing in Publication

Dublin, Anne, author
44 hours or strike! / by Anne Dublin.

Issued in print and electronic formats.
ISBN 978-1-927583-76-0 (paperback).—ISBN 978-1-927583-77-7 (epub)

1. Strikes and lockouts—Clothing trade—Ontario—Toronto—History—Juvenile fiction.
2. Women clothing workers—Ontario—Toronto—History—Juvenile fiction.
3. Women's rights—Ontario—Toronto—History—Juvenile fiction.
4. Employee rights—Ontario—Toronto—History—Juvenile fiction.
I. Title. II. Title: Forty-four hours or strike!.

PS8557.U233F68 2015   jC813'.6   C2015-903299-7

C2015-903300-4

Copyright © 2015 by Anne Dublin

Edited by Gena Gorrell
Copyedited by Karen Helm
Cover by Luc Normandin
Designed by Melissa Kaita

Printed and bound in Canada

This book is a work of fiction. Names, characters, and incidents either
are the product of the author's imagination or are used fictitiously.

The author gratefully acknowledges the support of the Ontario Arts Council.

*Second Story Press gratefully acknowledges the support of the
Ontario Arts Council and the Canada Council for the Arts for our
publishing program. We acknowledge the financial support of the
Government of Canada through the Canada Book Fund.*

MIX
Paper from
responsible sources
FSC
www.fsc.org   FSC® C004071

Published by
SECOND STORY PRESS
20 Maud Street, Suite 401
Toronto, ON M5V 2M5
www.secondstorypress.ca

For my beloved Aunt Pola z"l,
who taught me the meaning of work
and the joy of chocolate éclairs

Awake!
How long will you stand
With your backs bent low,
Humbled, homeless, and wan?
It dawns! Awake and open your eyes!
And feel your iron might!

David Edelstadt (1866–1892)

Toronto (1930s)

1 Balfour Building, 119 Spadina Ave.

2 Claremont police station, Bathurst St. & Queen St. W.

3 Mount Sinai Hospital, 100 Yorkville Ave.

4 Mercer Reformatory, King Street W. & Fraser Ave.

5 United Bakers Dairy Restaurant, 338 Spadina Ave.

6 The Labor Lyceum, 346 Spadina Ave.

7 The Jewish Old Folks' Home, 29 Cecil St.

8 Walerstein's Ice Cream Parlour, 332 Spadina Ave.

9 Lansdowne Public School, 33 Robert St.

10 Koffler's Drugstore, 376 College St.

11 Holy Blossom Synagogue, 115 Bond St.

12 Bellevue Square Park

13 Centre Island

A LITTLE HISTORY
TO EXPLAIN THIS STORY

In the late 1800s and early 1900s, the Russian Empire covered much of Eastern Europe. It was ruled by the tsar and a wealthy group of nobles who enjoyed great luxury while workers lived in poverty. Jewish people suffered more than most, being persecuted for their religion, and sometimes robbed, attacked, or even killed in savage anti-Semitic raids called pogroms.

Workers in Eastern Europe, including some Jews, rebelled against these injustices. Some wanted to band together into unions, to fight for better pay and working conditions. Others wanted a "Communist" state in which the government controlled all property and distributed benefits equally among the citizens. These ideas spread around the world, and they alarmed people who owned property and were afraid of losing it.

As ocean travel became easier, many Europeans migrated to North America—often with empty pockets—to build a new life. They were sometimes unpopular in their new country because they looked different, spoke different languages, and had different customs. They were accused of bringing their rebellious ideas with them and plotting to overturn the North American way of life.

From 1914 to 1918, World War I—the "Great War"—devastated Europe. After the war, yet more immigrants flooded to North America, taking any jobs they could get. But in 1929 the world fell into the Great Depression. Companies collapsed and there were not enough jobs to go around. Millions of people were unemployed. Many were starving; many were homeless. The union movement grew stronger as desperate workers looked for some way to feed, clothe, and shelter their families.

Distrust and resentment of immigrants increased as other people blamed their difficulties on these "foreigners," especially Eastern Europeans who might have Communist ideas. The Jews were suspected most of all because, at a time when the great majority of North Americans were Christian, they seemed especially different. They had escaped Europe, but they still faced prejudice and persecution. To some people, they were just "not like us."

CHAPTER 1
In the Garment District

It was Tuesday afternoon—almost evening—on a cold, gray day in February 1931. The whir and clatter of machines dinned in Sophie's ears. Her right knee pressed against the lever of the sewing machine as the cotton material slid steadily, evenly, under her fingers. Her back was aching and her eyes were sore. Her nose was full of the stuffiness of the fabric, the dust from the cutting machine, and the sweat of other workers.

"Hurry up!" a raspy voice said in her ear. "You won't make your quota at this rate!"

Sophie kept her head down and tried to sew faster. She mustn't lose this job. Mama was counting on her. She couldn't see the needle as it raced through the fabric but her fingers kept pushing the cloth forward in the same motion. Faster! Faster! In spite of the cold room, sweat dripped from her forehead onto her cheeks. She couldn't take the time to wipe it away.

Sophie had heard that sometimes, when a worker sewed too quickly, a needle went right through her finger. But she couldn't slow down. She had to keep going. The foreman didn't care about her fingers, as long as she didn't get blood on the cloth. She didn't want to think about what might happen. She didn't want to think about anything. She had to keep going, going, going.

Garment workers used industrial models
of the Singer sewing machine.

A heavy hand pressed on her shoulder. "I said hurry up!" a voice snarled. Sophie glanced up to see Mr. Fen, the foreman—a thin man with a beaky nose and small, dark eyes like a weasel's.

He squeezed her shoulder and she winced, but she didn't dare shake his hand off. She remembered stories she'd heard of girls doing "favors" for him in order to get jobs that paid better. She felt like a helpless mouse with Mr. Fen, the cat that was ready to pounce.

When he finally took his hand away, she spared a moment to take out her handkerchief and wipe the sweat from her face and neck. Her cotton blouse was sticking to her back, making her itchy and uncomfortable. The dust clogged her throat, and her eyes burned and watered. With all this, and the deafening noise, she felt unreal, as if she were caught in a waking nightmare.

Then, suddenly, a whistle pierced the racket. The machines stopped, one after another. Silence, blessed silence—except for the weary sighs of the workers, the cracking of joints as they stood up, and an occasional release of wind from women and girls who had been sitting for far too many hours.

Sophie tried to stand up but her legs shook. She sank back down on the chair, then gripped the sewing machine table and pushed herself up.

"Are you coming?" A young woman with pale skin and curly brown hair walked up to Sophie and put her arm around her. "Come on, little sister."

"I'm not little. I'm fourteen," Sophie said. "Just because you're two years older..." She rubbed the back of her neck.

"Every part of me is aching—from my head to my feet!"

Rose was used to working at the factory. Sophie had been there only a week, but it felt like twenty. It had been hard for her to get this job. Mama had had to beg the owner, Mr. Fox, once, twice, even three times. He had resisted, arguing that times were hard and he couldn't afford to hire more workers, but he'd finally agreed to give Sophie a chance. Papa had been a good worker, and Mr. Fox felt sorry for the family now that his death had left them to fend for themselves.

The workers called Mr. Fox "Foxy-Loxy" behind his back because he was always convinced that the sky was falling and he'd go bankrupt any minute. Mr. Fen's nickname was "Fenny-Penny" because he was always trying to squeeze every penny out of the girls (or trying to give them other kinds of squeezes).

The two sisters followed the other workers to the coat racks. Sophie put on Mama's old coat, which she'd borrowed to go to work: medium-gray wool with a fur collar. She remembered how happy Mama had been when Papa had bought it for her. "My wife should be dressed like a queen, not in *shmatas*, rags," he had said as he helped her put it on. Mama's face had glowed with love and pride.

Sophie wrapped the coat tightly around her, but she still shivered in the draft of icy air coming through the elevator door. She remembered the summer before Papa died. It had been a humid July evening without a breath of wind. "Let's go to Sunnyside Beach!" Papa had called when he came home from the factory. "A bunch of the men are taking their families and we'll all get together there."

Mama was cooking borscht in the summer kitchen, the screened porch off their second-story flat. There was an extra stove there that she used when it was too hot to cook inside. She stopped stirring and held the wooden spoon up like a weapon. "What? Just like that?"

"Why not?" Papa walked up to her and put his arm around her waist. "We'll take pillows and blankets, a little something to eat and drink, and we'll catch the streetcar down to the lake."

"A little something to eat and drink," Mama muttered, as she shook his arm off. "Now look what you made me do! The borscht is dripping all over the floor!" She went back to stirring the soup but looked over her shoulder. "And then what?"

"We'll sleep there all night!"

"On the sand? Near the water?"

"Of course on the beach! Where else?"

Sophie and Rose pulled on Mama's apron strings. "Let's do it, Mama! Let's go!"

Mama stared at Papa and the two girls, then shrugged and smiled faintly. "What can I do? It's three against one."

So they had packed their stuff and dragged it onto a streetcar filled with other people heading down to Sunnyside, and spent a wonderful night under a dark velvet sky. The murmuring people, the lapping of the waves, and the fresh breeze from the lake had all lulled Sophie into a dreamless sleep.

Now she tried to shake the memories away. They only distracted her, filling her with longing and despair. She had to concentrate on what she should do right now.

She followed the other girls and women onto the elevator.

The operator, a thin, wizened old man who said little as he sat on his stool in the corner, closed the two sliding doors and pressed the button. The elevator descended slowly to street level, and the two sisters walked out of the Balfour Building. Other workers were streaming out of the Fashion Building, a short block north of their intersection. This was the heart of Toronto's "garment district," where poor people spent long hours producing clothes they could not afford to buy.

Rose linked her arm in Sophie's as they walked along the sidewalk. "I hate these short winter days when we have to go to work in the dark and come home in the dark," she said. "And it'll be a lot darker by the time we get out of the union meeting at the Lyceum. But we have to go."

Sophie gulped the fresh air, and the fuzziness in her head began to clear. As they passed a boy selling newspapers on the corner, she stopped to glance at the *Toronto Daily Star*.

"Do you want a paper?" the boy asked. "It's only two cents." He was tall and lanky, and curly red hair peeked out from under his woolen cap. His blue eyes seemed to size her up, but Sophie saw kindness there too. And maybe curiosity.

She groped inside her empty pockets and shook her head apologetically. "No thanks."

The boy smiled at her. "Well, let me know if you change your mind. My name's Jake Malone and this is my corner."

She smiled back at him. "I will. Thanks."

Rose pulled Sophie's arm. "Sophie, come on! I want to get a seat at the meeting before they're all taken."

"Can't you wait a minute? I just want to talk to that boy."

The Balfour Building anchored the corner of Spadina
and Adelaide in the city's garment district. Rose and Sophie
worked long hours under hard conditions here.

Rose looked at Jake and pulled harder on her arm. "We've got to go. I mean it. *Right now.*"

"I'm coming. You don't have to be so bossy, Rose." Sophie glanced back at Jake, thinking he wanted to say something to her, but he just shook his head and raised his hand to say good-bye.

The sidewalks were jammed with people making their way home from work, while horses and wagons, cars and trucks, streetcars and vans fought their way along Spadina.

As the girls hurried on, Rose said, "I'm sorry I dragged you away. Are you mad at me? You must feel exhausted."

Sophie shrugged. "I'm okay."

"The factory takes some getting used to—the noise, the bad air, the long hours, the backbreaking work." Rose sighed and put her arm around her sister's shoulders. "Listen—do you understand why the union meeting is so important?"

Sophie looked at her. "I don't think so. But I guess I'm going to find out real soon."

Rose dropped her arm and trudged along the slushy sidewalk. She wished she'd been able to stay in school, but it had been impossible. Two years ago, during the slow season, Papa had been laid off. There was little money coming in. As the older daughter, Rose had to go to work. At first she'd thought it might be fun to have a job and be independent. Now she knew she had been wrong. If she'd stayed in school, she could have gone to business college. Eventually she could have found a decent job in an office. Instead, she was slaving away in a dress factory for lousy wages in awful working conditions.

Since she had started working, life had only gotten worse. First there was the big stock market crash, in the fall of 1929, when so many companies collapsed and so many people lost their jobs. And then, about a year later, Papa had died. They had known he was ill, but they had all pretended to each other that, somehow, he would get better. And now Mama was sick, and poor Sophie had to work in the factory too, and—oh, how would they ever make a better life?

Some days, Rose felt completely miserable. Other days, she still dared to make plans for the future. She would take night classes (when she wasn't too tired). She would find a wonderful job. She would marry a rich man. She was going to climb out of the rut she was in, if she had to use her teeth and nails to do it!

But now all she felt was anger. Everything kept getting worse and worse. They were trapped in their hopeless life.

CHAPTER 2

A Mound of Ashes

"Pipe down, everyone!" The man at the front of the hall at the Labor Lyceum could barely be heard above the din of hundreds of people greeting each other, laughing, and arguing. He banged his gavel on the table. "Quiet! Please! This union meeting will now come to order!"

The hall smelled of coffee and cigarettes, of floor cleaner and sweat. Tattered posters on the walls, in English and Yiddish, proclaimed slogans like "STAND TOGETHER WITH THE UNION" and "UNITED WE STAND, DIVIDED WE FALL."

Sophie sank down on a chair beside Rose.

The man whacked his gavel again. He was slender and of medium height, with stooped shoulders and a balding head. His lips were thin and he wore wire-rimmed glasses. As the crowd gradually quieted down, he began to speak. "My fellow workers, in case you don't know who I am—"

"We all know you, Mr. Shane!" someone shouted, and there was scattered laughter and applause.

The man held up his hand and waited for everyone to quiet down again. "I'm Bernard Shane, the international organizer of your union."

The crowd cheered.

He held up his hand again. "Your *GREAT* union—the ILGWU!"

Another cheer erupted. Sophie was wondering if the posters would fall down from all the vibrations, when Rose whispered in her ear, "The International Ladies' Garment Workers Union."

"We Jews came to Canada," Shane said, "to Montreal, to Toronto, and to Winnipeg, to escape the poverty and persecution we suffered in Eastern Europe." He spoke softly but everyone's eyes were fixed upon him. "Even if you never experienced those times—the pogroms, the cruelty—you've heard about them from your parents, your neighbors, your friends, or your fellow workers."

People nodded and whispered among themselves.

"We came here to make a better life for ourselves and for our families." Shane raised his voice. "Instead, what did we find?"

"Long hours!"

"Low wages!"

"Piecework!"

The union wanted all the garments
sewn by Rose and Sophie to carry this label.

"Speedups!"

"Dirty factories!"

"Too much work!"

"Too little work!"

"Getting fired for no reason!"

"The boss has his favorites!"

Shane let people go on calling out their grievances until the hubbub died down. "We found all that, and more," he continued, leaning over the lectern as he wagged his finger at them. "Remember what Abraham Cahan wrote." He rustled some papers. "He said, 'America has turned me into a mound of ashes.'"

A woman sitting in front of Sophie and Rose took out her handkerchief and wiped her eyes. "Who knew it would be so hard to make a living?" She blew her nose and crumpled her handkerchief into a soggy ball.

"Take it easy, Sadie," said the woman sitting beside her.

"Ethel, what are we going to do? How will we manage?"

"We'll just have to wait and see."

"Yeah," Sadie said, "like always."

Shane raised his fist in the air. "Why must we always take the streetcar or walk? Why must our children sit at home? Surely we are entitled to ride in a secondhand automobile, and go to a picture show now and then?"

"Of course we are!" a man shouted.

"That's Herman the Cutter," Rose whispered. "Beside him is his friend, Morris the Presser. They make a lot more money than we do."

"We produce the finest clothing in the world," Shane said, "yet we are working a thirteen-hour day—a seventy-hour-week—for starvation wages!" He sighed. "My good people, it is an intolerable situation."

"We're lucky to have the fare for the streetcar," Herman yelled.

"He's right!" Morris said.

Shane raised his hand for silence. He looked at the exhausted faces of the workers sitting on the folding metal chairs. He took a deep breath and let it out slowly. "The union has asked the employers for the following: a forty-four-hour week, a 15 percent increase in wages, and, most important of all, the right to bargain on behalf of all the workers." He gazed at the audience as if he could see right into their hearts. "The employers have refused."

Rose leaned over and whispered in Sophie's ear, "Wouldn't it be something if we didn't have to work on weekends? If we had decent lunch breaks and coffee breaks? If we even had time off if we were sick or—" she chuckled, "—when we had babies?"

Sophie shook her head. "You're dreaming."

Rose shrugged. "Maybe yes, maybe no."

"The time is now!" Shane pounded his fist on the lectern and pointed to the posters on the wall. "For I tell you: united we stand, divided we fall!" He paused and then, in a firm voice, said, "I ask your vote for a strike!"

"Strike! Strike! Strike!" the crowd chanted.

"Wait a minute!" Sadie raised a reddened hand and stood up. "How can I go on strike? I've got an unemployed husband

and three small children to support." She twisted her handkerchief. "How will I put food on the table? Who will pay the rent? How will I buy coal for my stove?" She sat down heavily.

"She's right," Herman said.

"We're all in the same boat," added Morris.

Everyone was shouting at the same time. Sophie put her hands to her ears. She'd always hated noisy places, and now she wished she could run out of the Lyceum, away from this unruly crowd. But she knew she'd have to stay there until the strike vote was taken and the decision was made. She had to stay for Rose, and for Mama. Most of all, she had to stay for herself.

Shane held up his hand and the voices died down. "Brothers and sisters, I know it will be hard. All of us will have to make sacrifices."

"So what else is new?" Herman shouted.

"You can't get blood from a stone," muttered Morris.

"Good people, please sit down and listen," Shane continued. "If we strike, I can assure you that the union will get financial support from the Workmen's Circle, from the Labor Zionists, and from other unions too. And of course you'll get moral support."

"You can't eat moral support," Sadie mumbled.

"If we stand together, we will win this fight." Shane leaned on the lectern. "Now, I ask you again. Does the union have your support for a strike? Here is the place! Now is the time!"

"Then let's strike!" Herman shouted.

"Of course we'll strike," Morris agreed. "Did you think for a second that we wouldn't?"

17

The crowd cheered, shouted, and finally cast their ballots. The vote was counted. Almost everyone had voted for a strike.

And yet, despite Shane's promises, Sophie wondered what would happen when they went out on strike. How long would the strike last? Did they have a chance of winning against the employers? Would those other groups really give them help to see them through?

Mama had very little money saved. How would they manage to eat, to pay the rent, to stay warm? If Mama got sicker, who would pay the doctor bills? And what if Mama—oh no, she couldn't bear to think about that.

Her head was spinning with worries. She had always thought she was an optimist, good at seeing the bright side of things, but it was hard to feel positive when everything was so awful. And she had a feeling it was going to get a lot worse before it got better.

CHAPTER 3
United We Stand

After the meeting at the Lyceum, Sophie and Rose linked arms and walked to their second-floor flat on Robert Street. The house was a thirty-minute walk north from the factory, but that's why Mama had been able to get it for a cheaper rent. The street was far enough away from Kensington Market that Sophie didn't have to hold her breath when the window was open in good weather. She hated the smells of horse droppings and rancid fish, of live chickens and rotten fruit and vegetables from the outdoor stalls.

The narrow house was packed close to identical ones on the street. A dirty patch of snow lay on the tiny front yard, as if it couldn't decide whether to melt or wait for more snow to join it. Behind the house was an alley where kids sometimes played and cats yowled at night. All the houses looked sad and run-down. No one had money anymore to buy paint, or to repair leaky roofs and sagging porches.

The girls plodded up the stairs, turned the key in the lock, and pushed the door open. "It's been a long day," Rose sighed, as they hung their hats and coats on hooks in the tiny vestibule. The air smelled of boiled cabbage, fried onions, and damp clothes.

Mama was lying on the couch in the front room, a hot-water bottle on her stomach. Various bottles and jars were scattered on a side table. As Sophie walked closer, she could smell the pungent odor of liniment. She wanted to open a window, but coal for the stove was expensive. Mama would yell, "We're not heating the whole city!"

Mama tried to sit up when she heard the girls come in, but groaned as she plopped down again upon the pillows. Her eyes were too bright; her face looked waxy and pale. Sophie had a sick feeling in the pit of her stomach. She always worried that Mama would die too; that she and Rose would be left alone in the world. She tried to push the thought away but couldn't.

Mama waved toward the kitchen. "I made some potato soup for you. It's on the stove. I hope it's still warm."

"Do you want some, Mama?" Rose asked.

Mama shook her head. "I have no appetite." She gestured to Sophie. "Come here, child."

Sophie went to the couch and sat down gingerly at Mama's feet. She smelled the musty odor of old clothes. Mama was just forty years old, but she looked sixty. Sophie pushed back her gnawing fear that she too would grow old before her time, before she'd really lived.

Mama leaned over and stroked her daughter's hair. "How was it at the factory today? Are you getting used to the work?"

"It was all right, I guess." Mama looked so frail, as if she might disappear any minute. Sophie bit her lip. "You really should eat something."

"I can't. My stomach hurts every time I eat."

"What does the doctor say?"

Her mother shrugged. "Who has money for doctors?"

Rose walked over to the couch and wrinkled her nose. "Maybe you'll have a bath tonight?"

But Mama shook her head. "Not tonight. I feel too weak." She shooed the girls away. "Go. Eat something. And sit at the table!" Then she grimaced and handed Sophie the hot-water bottle. "Put the kettle on and fill it for me, *shepseleh*." She doubled over in pain. "Don't worry—I'll be all right."

That night, the girls were lying on the pullout couch they shared in the front room. Sophie yawned. "I'm so tired I could sleep forever!" She nudged Rose. "Like Sleeping Beauty."

"And you maybe expect a prince to come along?"

"Why not?"

Rose nudged her back. "Somehow, I don't think princes are interested in Jewish factory girls."

"Who knows? This is Canada. Anything is possible."

"You sound like Papa!"

"Do I?" Sophie yawned again. "I guess I do."

"I wish he were here. Tomorrow will be a big day," Rose whispered. "I'm supposed to announce the strike at the factory."

"You? Why you? When?"

"Mr. Shane noticed me at the meeting. He pulled me aside and asked me to, while I was waiting for you. When you were in the washroom."

"But Rose, you're just…a girl."

"Maybe so, but I know how to fight for what's right."

"And if you get into trouble?"

"I won't."

"But if you do?"

"Then I do. *Someone* has to fight to change things!"

"But shouldn't we tell Mama?"

"There will be plenty enough time for that. Go to sleep, little sister."

Although Sophie's head was filled with worries, she was soon fast asleep.

✂

Rose walked over to the main power switch and pulled the lever. The lights went out and all the machines stopped. The room grew silent and dim, with only the faint winter light filtering through the dusty windows. It lit up a worried face here, a dusty machine there, and piles of fabric and spools of thread.

"Stand up, everyone! Stop work!" Rose shouted. "It's time

to go on strike!" She reached into the pocket of her skirt, took out a folded piece of paper, and flourished it. "Here's what Bernard Shane said: 'Every operator, finisher, cutter, presser, and draper must stop work at exactly ten o'clock on Wednesday, February 25 and march to the Lyceum hall. Leave your shop orderly and do not create any disturbances.'" She shoved the paper back into her pocket. "The time has come for action!"

All around Sophie, women stood up, tidied their work areas, grabbed their purses, and headed for the coat racks.

Suddenly, Mr. Fen was blocking the door and holding a big bucket of water. "You're not going anywhere!" he screamed. "Are you crazy? A strike? Mr. Fox will never stand for this!"

A young woman walked past Fen and called back over her shoulder, "Who cares about Fox?"

"That's the way, Becky!" Rose cried.

Becky pointed a finger at Mr. Fen. "Fox sits in his fancy house and drives his fancy car and eats his fancy food." She snapped her fingers. "He used to be one of us, but he doesn't give a hoot about us anymore!"

"I'm warning you…" Fen said.

"Humph!" said Becky. "Warn away!"

Mr. Fen raised the bucket and threw cold water all over her.

"Are you crazy?" gasped Becky. Her hair was dripping and her clothes were drenched.

"She'll catch her death of cold!" Rose protested.

"It serves her right." Fen put the bucket down and stood solidly in the doorway, his arms crossed on his chest. "Now—all of you—get back to your machines."

A few workers began to dry Becky off, but she wasn't through yet. "Do you think a little cold water is going to stop us?" She beckoned to the others. "Come on, girls. Let's get out of here!"

"You'll be sorry!" Fen shouted as they shoved him out of the way. "You'll be out of work, all of you. There are lots of other girls who'll be glad to take your jobs."

As they hurried out of the building, Sophie tried to make herself small in the crowd. Her heart pounded as she joined the stream of workers walking along Spadina toward the Lyceum.

"That's the way to deal with them!" Herman the Cutter said.

"We're not going to let the bosses take advantage of us!" added Morris the Presser.

Sophie thought how strange the two men looked as they marched side by side. Herman was tall and thin while Morris was short and stout. Both had the pale complexions of people who had worked indoors for years on end. They constantly argued about politics. They called each other names and swore at each other with colorful Yiddish curses. They rarely agreed about anything, but they were the best of friends.

"Why are you walking out of a good job when there are plenty of people begging for work?" wondered a bystander, when he heard what was happening.

"You're a bunch of Commie Jews!" shouted another man, as he spit on the sidewalk. "You want to take the food out of good Canadian mouths!"

"Yeah," shouted a third as he elbowed his way through the

gathering crowd. "You should tighten your belts, like everyone else." Other shouts and insults followed.

"You women should stay home where you belong. You're taking jobs away from decent, hardworking men who need to support their families."

"Go back to the kitchen, that's what I say!"

"I'll go in there right now," said a tall, scrawny man. "I'll show them that I can do your job better than you can."

"Then you'll be a lousy strike-breaker!" Herman shouted.

"A scab is the lowest of the low!" Morris yelled.

As Sophie and Rose passed Jake, the newspaper boy, he took off his cap and scratched his head. Sophie heard him mutter, "I wonder what Pa would say." He put his cap back on and shook his head. "He'd probably think they're crazy to go on strike. But I wonder if he's right."

Sophie didn't want to admit it, but she wondered who was right too.

Women and girls who worked in the garment factories took to the
streets to picket for better wages and working conditions.

CHAPTER 4
Divided We Fall

It was the tenth day since the strike began. A small group of people were carrying placards and walking quietly back and forth in front of the garment factories at the corner of Spadina and Adelaide. One of the picketers started singing the Yiddish words to a song called "The Internationale," and the others joined in.

Shteyt oyf, ir ale ver vi shklafn,
in hunger lebt ir un in noyt.
Der geyst, er kokht, er ruft tsum vafn—
in shlakht undz firn iz er greyt.

Arise, you workers from your slumber!
Arise, you wretched of the earth!
Don't cling so hard to your possessions,
For you have nothing if you have no rights!

Some unemployed men loitered on the street, smoked, and made small talk. A few policemen stood near the intersection, and one policeman on horseback rode back and forth.

The sky was gray and there was the feeling of impending snow in the air. In spite of this, in nearby Kensington Market, storekeepers were opening their shops and piling boxes filled with fruit and vegetables in front of their windows, or big barrels of herring or pickles beside their doors. Old women in heavy shawls or worn jackets sat on stools and plucked slaughtered

Kensington Market was a hub of activity where shoppers could find almost anything—from live poultry to hardware.

chickens. Other chickens and ducks clucked and squawked in their cages, waiting for their turn. The various smells of produce and fish, herring and pickles, chickens and spices were overpowering.

The side streets were clogged with peddlers collecting things like scrap metal or rags to sell to junkyards or paper-making plants. Trucks were parked everywhere, and some merchants were selling too-ripe bananas off the backs of their beat-up trucks.

Cars, trucks, and an occasional horse-drawn wagon moved slowly along the wide street. Crowded streetcars clanged on the tracks, taking people to work. In front of the Balfour Building, a taxi stopped and four women got out.

Herman the Cutter muttered, "Look at them—strikebreakers! The bosses must have paid for the taxi."

"They've got money for taxis but not for decent wages for us," Morris added.

The women looked nervously at the strikers marching in front of the building, and huddled together as they made their way toward the picket line.

One of them was a woman in her forties with a lined face and graying hair. She wore a threadbare gray coat that she hugged to her body, with gloves so worn that her fingers poked through. Becky stalked over to her. "Kathleen, I know you. Don't cross our picket line. Don't do this to us!"

"Becky Levy, get out of my way!" said the woman. "I got kids to feed. One's home sick with the croup. I need to buy medicine and pay for the doctor."

She began to push past the picketers, but Becky grabbed her arm. "Kathleen, if you go in, you'll make it worse for all of us."

Kathleen shook her hand off. "Let me pass! You got no right to tell me what to do!"

"We're fighting for better working conditions," Becky argued, as the picketers crowded closer to the two women. "For a decent wage. For our union."

"It's not just for us," Rose added.

"We're striking for everyone," Becky said.

Kathleen frowned. "I don't care! I got to feed my family. Besides, you never cared about us English workers. At least, not before you wanted us to join the strike." She spit as she talked. "Your meetings are always in Yiddish, so we can't even understand what's going on. And all the big shots in the union are Jewish too." She paused to take a breath. "If you cared about us at all, you would've tried harder, talked English, included us more." She took a step forward. "Now let me pass!"

"That's not true!"

Kathleen sneered, "Isn't it, now?" She elbowed her way through the strikers. "I'm going into the factory. And don't try to stop me! Besides, I'm not the only one." She pointed behind her. "My friend Irene is here, and others too."

The other women who had come by taxi pushed through the crowd and stood beside Kathleen. The two lines faced each other—the picketers on one side, the strike-breakers on the other. They stood rigid and tense, like two hockey teams waiting for a face-off.

"We have to work," Kathleen said.

"We got no choice," said Irene.

"But you *do* have a choice!" said Rose. "We all do."

"I won't let you go in!" Becky said.

"I won't either!" Rose spread her arms out, trying to block the women.

"Just try to stop me!" Kathleen shoved Becky aside.

Becky pushed her back, and Kathleen fell down hard onto the sidewalk. "Have you no respect?" she yelled.

"An older woman, and look what you did!" said Irene.

"You should be ashamed!" agreed a man in the crowd, helping Kathleen up.

Becky backed away, her red face a mixture of defiance and embarrassment. "I *had* to do something!" She faced the crowd. "I had to protect our jobs."

"What trouble are you strikers making now?" A burly policeman pushed his way through the crowd, and beckoned to the policeman on horseback.

"Watch out, Sophie," Rose whispered. "It's O'Brien. He's a real anti-Semite!"

Kathleen was back on her feet with her hands on her hips. "She pushed me down. She was going to punch me too," she said to the two policemen.

"I was not!" Becky shouted.

Rose stepped forward and stood beside Becky. "We were only trying to stop her from crossing the picket line."

O'Brien grabbed Becky by the arm. "Come along now. We'll not have you making trouble on the streets of Toronto."

"I wasn't—"

"You'd better come quietly or—"

"Leave her alone!" cried Rose. "She didn't do anything wrong!"

O'Brien grabbed Rose. "And you too, miss. We'll not have you disturbing the peace."

"Rose!" Sophie yelled.

By now, mounted police were pushing the crowd back. Other police used billy clubs to beat people on the head, arms, anywhere they could. Someone pushed Sophie and she fell down, hitting her head on the sidewalk.

Becky and Rose were arrested for disorderly conduct, for "creating a disturbance by using insulting language." Rose thought it was good the police couldn't understand the Yiddish curses she had been yelling at them, or she would have been in even more trouble. She and Becky were shoved into the back seat of a police car.

As they were driven away, Rose looked out the window and saw people crowding around Sophie. Someone was helping her get up. Rose hoped she was all right. She felt guilty that she hadn't protected her sister, and wondered what Sophie would say to their mother, and how the two of them would manage without her. She felt her throat tighten and tears came to her eyes. She was shivering with cold and fear, and felt much younger than her sixteen years. "What's going to happen to us?"

Her voice was trembling as she tried not to cry.

Becky shrugged. "I don't know. But remember, we didn't do anything wrong."

"I guess that's why we were arrested, huh?"

Becky snorted. "We all know the cops are on the side of the owners. Just because they call us labor agitators doesn't mean we did anything wrong."

"Why do they hate us so much?"

"Probably for stirring up trouble in Toronto the Good." Becky put her arm around Rose's shoulders. "And maybe because we're Jewish. They don't understand us, so they hate us."

Rose took a big breath. "I know. The union is our only hope to make changes, to better our lives."

"What else could we do?"

They were taken to the Claremont Street police station and locked in separate cold, damp cells in the basement. The walls and floor were brick; the small, high window had thick iron bars. The only furniture was an iron cot, a table and chair bolted to the floor, and a bucket to use as a toilet.

Rose sat on the edge of the cot and wondered what would happen next. She was hungry and thirsty. She put her elbows on her knees and her pounding head in her hands, and began to rock back and forth, back and forth. She pretended she was home, back in Mama's arms like a little girl being rocked to sleep. She tried to remember the words of the lullaby Mama had sung to her:

Unter Rushkele's vigele
Shteyt a klor-vays tsigele.

Dos tsigele iz geforn handlen
Dos vet zayn dayn baruf.
Rozhinkes mit mandlen.
Shlof-zhe, Rushkele, shlof.

Under Rose's cradle
Stands a small white goat.
He traveled far to sell his wares.
And Rose will travel too.
Selling raisins, selling almonds.
Sleep, Rose, sleep.

She couldn't lie down on the cot, with its rusty springs and moldy mattress. She was sure there must be bedbugs in there. Every spring and fall, Mama cleaned the mattresses with kerosene to get the bugs out. Rose had the feeling this mattress was a bedbugs' holiday. Not to mention the cockroaches hiding in the corner. She shivered. She'd always been disgusted by creepy-crawlies.

After what seemed like hours, a woman in a gray dress unlocked the door of the cell. She followed closely behind Rose as they walked up the stairs and along a hallway. The woman knocked on a door, opened it, and pushed Rose inside. Then she stood near the door, as if she were afraid Rose might make a run for it.

Rose was so scared that her legs were shaking. She could barely stand.

The small room was empty of furniture except for a desk

and chair, a phone, and a typewriter. Another woman sat behind the desk. She looked up from her typewriter but barely gave Rose a glance. "Name?" She spoke loudly, as if Rose couldn't hear or understand.

"Rose Abramson."

"How old are you?"

"Sixteen."

The woman jotted her answer down. "Religion?"

"Jewish."

Her lips curled in disdain. "Father?"

Rose swallowed hard. "He died last year."

"Mother?"

"She's home but she's sick."

"I didn't ask for your life story," the woman snapped. "Just tell me your mother's name and your address."

Rose felt her face growing red, but she answered the woman's questions as politely as she could.

Finally the woman stopped typing and stared at Rose with cold blue eyes. "You've been charged with vagrancy." She tapped the desk with her pencil. "I'll give this information to the magistrate shortly." She waved her hand. "Take her away."

The guard pushed her toward a small waiting room and pointed at the solitary chair. Rose stared at the picture of King George V on the wall. She could not think anymore. She just sat there waiting, waiting for whatever would be.

The guard led Rose into a courtroom and told her to stand facing the judge, who was sitting on a raised seat on a kind of platform. The judge asked her the same questions the woman behind the desk had asked. He paused for about ten seconds, and then sentenced her to thirty days at the Mercer Reformatory for Women or a hundred-dollar fine—as if she had ever seen that much money in her life!

The guard led her downstairs to street level and put her in the back of a police car. The doors were locked. She looked out the window at the dark street. What was this Mercer Reformatory? What would they do to her there? She had never been so terrified in her life.

She remembered her parents' high hopes when they'd come to Toronto ten years before. She remembered Papa explaining to her, "I came to Canada to make a living. Back in Russia, it was impossible. We Jews couldn't move from one place to another. We were stuck like mice in a hole. If someone—and there were plenty of someones—wanted to beat us up or destroy our homes, no one would stop them. Finally, I decided enough was enough. It was time to go to America."

He had smiled one of his gap-toothed smiles. "How could I know that Canada wasn't America, where the streets are supposed to be paved with gold? But never mind. It's all right." He had gestured out the kitchen window. "In Toronto I may always be a pauper, but at least I'll be a *free* one!"

Papa had found a job right away as a presser in Fox's factory on Spadina Avenue. During the busy season, he used to work twelve-hour days, six days a week. He said he got Sunday off for good behavior—like a convict in prison. Then, if he wasn't too tired, the family would go to Walerstein's Ice Cream Parlour on Spadina Avenue. The girls would have sodas; Mama and

Papa would have tea. Or they'd ride the ferry to Centre Island in summer, when the weather was nice. Rose always liked the names of the ferries—the *Primrose* and the *Mayflower*. She liked to think of floating to the Island on a flower.

But that was before these hard times came, and people stopped buying new clothes. Before Papa got laid off and then got sick and died of tuberculosis.

She was sure it would have been the farthest thing from Papa's mind that either of his dear girls would ever get into trouble. But now Rose was on her way to the Mercer—the biggest trouble he could ever have imagined.

CHAPTER 5
Down to Earth

"Sophie!" Mama knocked on the bathroom door. "Are you all right?"

Sophie touched her fingers to her throbbing head and then stared at them. They were covered with sticky blood. She gagged and tasted sourness in her mouth. She always felt sick at the sight of blood. Papa had wanted her to become a nurse, but that was never going to happen.

As the memory of the day's events came flooding back to her, she sagged down on the toilet seat and pressed her hands to her head.

She had been knocked down by the mounted policeman and had lain sprawled on the dirty sidewalk for what seemed like hours. And then—

"Miss, can I help you?" As her blurred vision cleared, she saw that it was Jake, the paper boy. She moaned and tried to raise her head, but it felt as heavy as a boulder. Her hands were scraped and sore; her head was pounding. Still, she blushed and wondered what people would say—a fourteen-year-old girl lying on the filthy, slushy street.

Jake gave her his hand. She reached up and he pulled her gently to her feet. He tried to brush the slush and mud off her coat but only spread it around. She realized that he was avoiding her eyes. He must be as embarrassed as I am, she thought.

As Sophie stood there, dazed, Ethel and Sadie rushed over and huddled around her.

"Are you all right?" Ethel asked.

"I think so."

Sadie glanced at Jake and said firmly, "She'll be okay now."

"Are you sure?" Jake looked at Sophie and then at the women. He kicked at a pile of dirty snow on the sidewalk with the toe of his boot.

"Yes, I'm all right now," Sophie said.

"She's sure," echoed Ethel.

Sophie touched Jake on the arm. "Thanks for your help." She tried to smile. "Anyway, you probably have to get back to work."

He kicked at the snow again. His boot was scuffed and Sophie could see a hole at the bottom. "Yeah. I'd better get back to my crummy papers."

As the women pulled Sophie away, she called, "See you!"

Jake picked up his newspapers from the *Toronto Daily Star* building, then sold them by hand near Spadina and Adelaide. Other newsboys sold papers from a stand like this one at King and Yonge.

He nodded. "Yeah. See you." Under his breath he added, "I hope."

✄

"Sophie?" Mama knocked on the door again. "Can I come in?"

Sophie shook her head but winced at the movement. "No! You can't!"

"But—"

"I'll be right out."

When she heard Mama's footsteps fade down the hall, she got up and washed her hands and face. The girl in the mirror looked normal—same curly brown hair, same hazel eyes—but she wondered what normal was. How normal was it to almost get trampled by a horse? Her head was still pounding and the whole world seemed to be turning upside down.

She pressed a wet washcloth to her forehead. She forced herself to drink a glass of water and took a deep breath. She was as ready as she would ever be.

Sophie walked into the kitchen and sat down on a chair. Mama was standing at the stove, her back to Sophie. "I thought you might be hungry." She put a bowl of chicken soup with matzo balls on the table and suddenly Sophie felt ravenous. There's nothing like going on strike to give a person an appetite, she thought.

Mama was staring at Sophie. She clutched the edge of the table, her face going pale. "What happened?" She reached over and touched Sophie's head.

"Ow!"

"How did you get that bump on your head?"

"I banged it on the stupid door." She stared into her soup, not wanting to admit the lie she was telling.

"What door? Where?"

Sophie blew on the hot soup and spooned it into her mouth. It soothed her throat. "It doesn't matter."

"Are you all right?"

She swallowed another spoonful. "As all right as I'll ever be."

Mama paused and stared at her suspiciously. "Where's Rose? I didn't hear you come in. Didn't she come home with you? Was I sleeping?"

Sophie put her spoon down and raised her hands. "Stop with all the questions, Mama! I'll tell you, but it's not good news."

"Better an ounce of luck than a pound of gold," Mama muttered. "Tell me."

Sophie took a deep breath. "Rose is…she was taken…to the police station."

Mama gasped and sank down onto a chair. "*Gevalt!* The police station? Why? What are you talking about?"

"The police arrested some strikers. They took them to the station."

"The police station? My Rose?" Mama's face was so pale that Sophie was afraid she was going to faint. "I told her a million times not to get involved with the union," she wailed. "It's nothing but trouble!"

"But Mama—"

Mama shook her head. "Now look what's happened! Rose got arrested and you got hurt!" Her shoulders sagged and tears welled up in her eyes. She took her crumpled handkerchief out of her apron pocket and blew her nose. "If your Papa was here—"

Sophie stood up abruptly—too abruptly, because her head started to spin. "If Papa was here, I would still be in school," she said. "And so would Rose. We wouldn't need to slave in the factory and fight for better working conditions. We wouldn't have to march on the picket line and get beaten up by the police. We wouldn't—"

"Stop already!" Mama stood up and grabbed Sophie's shoulders. "We don't have a choice of what happens in life. We just have to accept it."

But Sophie shook Mama's hands off. "Well, *I* still have a choice. I don't have to accept this rotten situation."

Mama signed. "I have to go there. The police station. And you must come with me. You know I don't speak English very well. When I get upset, I forget the few words I know."

"But Mama, it's almost nighttime. Besides, they probably won't do anything until Monday."

Mama plopped back down on the chair. Her face looked drawn, with a look of defeat Sophie had never seen before.

Sophie's stomach clenched into knots. She had never been to a police station. She dreaded what they would find there. And now she would have to wait the whole weekend to find out.

Jake didn't have much time to think about Sophie. After he had sold the rest of his papers, he went home. Ma was ironing shirts for Mr. Fox, the owner of that dressmaking factory on Spadina. Pa was out somewhere.

Jake was glad. Things were always tense when Pa was home and griping about everything. He got a glass of milk from the icebox and sat down on a kitchen chair. His younger sisters, Nora and Ida, were playing checkers on the living-room floor.

Jake looked over at his mother. "Ma, what do you think about this dressmakers' strike?"

She glanced at him, brushed some stray hairs off her forehead, and tucked them into her kerchief. She spit on the iron to see if it was hot enough, and took another shirt out of her ironing basket.

"I don't really know what to think." She passed the iron over the collar and started a sleeve. Jake liked to smell the clean clothes and hear the hiss of the iron. He wished his problems could be smoothed out as easily as a shirt or a pair of pants.

"I guess I'd say," Ma began, "I don't think this is the time to strike." She paused. "On the other hand, when I was young, before I married, I had to work for a time in a weaving factory." She laid the other sleeve on the board. "Ah, but life was hard then! We worked from early morning until late at night, six days a week. On payday the owner always found a reason to dock our wages." She shook her head. "The unions weren't strong enough in those days to help us make things better. Not that I think a strike will help much now."

She started pressing the body of the shirt. "You know, I was glad to get married and escape that slave work." She placed the iron upright, put her hands on the small of her back, and stretched. "I know you don't get along so well with Pa—"

Jake snorted.

She held up her hand. "He's not perfect, but so many good men died in the war…"

Jake knew what she meant. She had not had much choice in husbands.

Ma shrugged. "Ah well. That's water under the bridge. Now go take your sisters for a walk so I can finish my ironing!"

"Ma—" Jake wanted to remind her that he had a big hole on the bottom of his shoe, but when he looked at her bent figure, he decided to keep quiet.

"Come on, little ones," he said to his sisters. "Clean up your game and we'll go to the park."

CHAPTER 6
At the Station

On Monday morning, Sophie helped Mama put on her coat—
the one Sophie had been wearing to work and on the picket
line—and then she put on her own old coat. She had outgrown
it so much that she could hardly do the buttons up.

Sometimes, when she was downtown, she looked at the
display windows at the Eaton's store. She wondered what it
would be like to have a warm woolen coat trimmed with fur
and lined with satin, and to walk along the sidewalk in warm,
dry boots. She was embarrassed that Mama owned only an old
coat, and a faded, old-fashioned shawl on her head.

She pointed to her mother's feet. "You forgot to take off
your slippers."

"Oy! What was I thinking?"

"Sit down, Mama. I'll help you."

Finally they were ready to leave. Mama locked the door, muttering, "As if there's anything here worth stealing!" Sophie helped her down the stairs to the street and half pulled, half carried Mama to the streetcar stop at the corner of College and Spadina. The Claremont Street police station was more than ten blocks away, and Mama was much too weak to walk. Sophie almost wished she could go alone, but she knew that Mama wouldn't let her.

"We can't afford the fare," Mama complained as they waited for the streetcar.

Streetcars ran up and down Spadina Avenue.

"You can't walk all the way to the police station." She turned her back to the biting wind. "The streets are too icy and the wind is too cold."

Mama sighed. "In my younger days, this would have been nothing. I remember back in Russia…"

They had to transfer streetcars and Sophie helped Mama out of one streetcar and onto another. When they got off at their stop, Mama had to pause to catch her breath every few minutes along the way. They reached the station and walked up the slippery stone steps, with Mama wincing in pain at every step.

Sophie found a seat for her mother on a wooden bench in the waiting room, and looked around. People were muttering and moaning, screaming and crying; typewriters were clacking; phones were ringing. She already hated the place, with its ugly green walls and strange smells. And Mama looked so out of place, huddled under her old shawl.

"Take off your shawl, Mama," Sophie whispered.

"What?"

"Your shawl."

Mama was oblivious to people's stares, and waved her daughter away. "Go, go! Talk to the policeman about our Rose."

Sophie's legs trembled as she walked up to the reception desk, where a husky policeman sat. His red hair was cropped above his ears. He had a small, flattish nose and a short, trimmed mustache. Above his high collar, his jowls jiggled as he talked on the phone and wrote furiously on a pad of paper. His nametag, pinned to the front of his dark blue jacket with its shiny brass buttons, read "A. Jones." To Sophie, everything about him screamed *goy*, non-Jew.

She felt rooted to the spot, too scared to speak. Her mouth was dry and her hands were clammy. Standing in front of the desk, she felt about two inches tall.

But then she remembered Rose. "Excuse me," she said.

Jones ignored her.

She stood on her tiptoes and said in a louder voice, "Excuse me, sir."

Jones put a hand over the mouthpiece and hissed, "Take a number. Sit down. I'll call you when it's your turn."

Sophie noticed numbers hanging on a holder on the desk. She took one and sat down beside Mama, wishing with all her heart that she had never come to this awful place.

After what seemed like hours, Officer Jones finally called Sophie's number. "Now, what will you be wanting?" His breath smelled of tobacco. "A young girl like you?"

"I…I…my sister was brought here."

"Oh?" He raised his eyebrows. "And why was that?"

"She…we…were on the picket line." Jones began to frown. Sophie cast her eyes down but then decided that she had nothing to be ashamed of, so she raised her chin. "You know, the dressmakers' strike."

Jones shook his head and wagged his finger. "No good will come of it, you know. It's hard times now and—"

"Please, can we see her?" Sophie looked back over her shoulder, to the bench where Mama was slumped. Her eyes were closed and she was breathing heavily. "I brought my mother with me. She's not well."

Jones glanced at Mama. "What's your sister's name?" He squinted at a sheaf of papers in front of him.

"Rose," Sophie said. "Rose Abramson."

He shuffled through the papers. Finally he looked up. "She's gone."

"Gone? What do you mean, gone?"

He looked at her and a faint smile played on his thick lips. "The judge gave the strikers thirty days in jail or a fine of one hundred dollars. She couldn't pay the fine, so they took her away."

Sophie felt as if the air had been knocked out of her. She licked her lips. "Where—where is she? Where did they take her?" she cried.

Jones raised his eyebrows. "Young lady, you needn't use that tone with me."

Sophie took a deep breath and tried to control her shaking voice. "Please, sir. Please tell me where she is."

"Let's see…" Jones held up a sheet of paper. "She was sent with the other vagrants to the Mercer Reformatory, the jail for women."

"But where's that?" Thoughts raced through her mind. Was Rose really in jail? Locked up in a cell? Like a criminal? It couldn't be true. It was too horrible. But what could she do?

"On King Street," Officer Jones was saying. "Did you hear me?"

"What?"

"The Mercer." He gestured vaguely. "It's on King Street."

Sophie wished she could sink to the floor. How was she ever going to get there? Let alone take Mama?

"Now, you should get yourself and your mother home. A girl your age—you shouldn't be here among all this riffraff. Get along with you."

Sophie nodded and made her way back to where she had left Mama. All she wanted at that moment was to get out of that crowded, noisy place and go home. She needed to decide what to do next. Who could she go to? Where could she get advice? Whom could she depend upon? Her head swirled with fear and indecision.

She explained the situation to Mama and helped her to her feet. Mama pulled her shawl back over her head. Sophie opened the heavy door and Mama clutched the railing as if it were a life preserver.

As they were going down the stairs, a boy and a woman were coming up. Sophie recognized Jake, the newspaper boy. He was saying, "Don't worry. Pa's probably drunk as usual. He'll be home before you know it."

Sophie didn't hear Jake say anything else because, at that moment, Mama slipped on a patch of ice. She slid down the stairs and lay sprawled in a dirty puddle of slush.

CHAPTER 7
More and More Alone

If a person is going to fall down and hurt herself, one of the best places to do it is in front of a police station. Quicker than you could say "potato kugel," a bunch of policemen and passersby crowded around Mama as she lay helpless at the bottom of the steps.

She tried to stand up but collapsed again. She kept repeating, "Oy! It hurts!" Her shawl had dropped to her shoulders; the pins in her bun had loosened and the wind was blowing her hair about. Her hands shook as she rubbed her ankle.

Sophie tried to help her stand up, but it was impossible. As thin as Mama had become, she was too heavy to lift. Sophie had no idea what to do. She felt like crying.

A hand touched her sleeve. "Sophie, let me help you."

Sophie looked up into Jake's eyes, and wondered how he knew her name. "Thank you," she whispered. How strange it was that when Mr. Fen had put his hand on her shoulder, she had been scared and nervous; when Jake did it, she felt warm and comforted.

Jake held Mama by one arm while a policeman held her by the other. Together, they managed to get her up the stairs and back into the station. Sophie grabbed Mama's battered purse and followed them.

They eased Mama down onto the bench.

Sophie sat down beside Mama and put an arm around her. "What do you want to do, Mama?"

The policeman looked over his shoulder as he made his way to the desk. "I'll phone for an ambulance."

"No! No ambulance. No doctors," cried Mama. "We can't afford it."

The policeman shrugged. "Fine," he muttered. "You don't know what's good for you!"

Sophie glared at the policeman. "Don't worry, Mama. We'll go to the Mount Sinai Hospital. You don't have to pay if you can't afford it. Besides, they speak Yiddish there."

"What about the *trayfe*, non-kosher food? I can't eat there! I'll starve to death!"

"Mama, it's a *Jewish* hospital. I'm sure the food is kosher. Besides, we don't know how long you'll have to stay there." She paused, hoping the next thing she said was true. "You probably just sprained your ankle. They'll fix it up and send you right home."

"It's the last stop before the cemetery!" Mama wailed. She took her handkerchief out of her pocket and wiped her eyes.

"Mama, you're being old-fashioned. People don't believe that anymore."

"I'll be all alone." Mama blew her nose.

"I'll stay with you until we know what's happening." Sophie stood up. "Now, will you please let me take you?"

Mama had finally run out of excuses. "A Jewish hospital." Her lips quivered. "All right. You win. I will go." She smiled faintly. "Who knows? Maybe I'll find a nice young doctor who will marry my Rose." Then she gasped and put her hand to her heart. "Rose! What will become of her?"

"One thing at a time, Mama. That's what you always say. Stay here while I ask a policeman to phone for a taxi."

Mama sighed. "I see my baby is growing up." She wadded up her handkerchief and shoved it back into her coat pocket.

"I'll stay with her until you come back," Jake said. Sophie gave him a quick smile.

She asked Officer Jones to call for a taxi, and then sat back down on the bench next to Mama and rubbed her back. Her hands shook and her head hurt. So far, this had been the worst day of her life. And it wasn't over yet.

Jake brought Mama a glass of water, and Sophie looked up into his kind eyes. "Thanks. You've been wonderful!"

"Thank you, young man," Mama said. She gulped the water down, handed the glass back to Jake, and closed her eyes. "Tell me when the taxi is here."

Jake sat down on Sophie's other side. His face was red and

he kept looking at her, and then down at his feet. "How's the strike going?" he asked.

"You care about the strike and what happens to us?"

"Well, yeah. Of course I do."

"Sorry. I didn't mean to insult you. It's only—"

"—You think people like me wouldn't understand what you're going through? Is that what you mean?"

"Well, you're not one of us." Sophie's mouth felt dry. "You're not—"

Jake's back stiffened. "Jewish? Is that it?"

"Well, you're not. Are you?" She was sorry she'd opened her big mouth. She was always accusing Rose of speaking too rashly. Now she was doing the same thing.

He stuck out his chin. "No. I'm not Jewish. I'm what you call a goy. Right?"

She nodded.

"But that doesn't make me less of a person."

Sophie shook her head. "Of course not! I didn't mean that at all." She touched his arm. "It's just…I thought no one else was on our side."

Jake looked down and put his hand on hers. He was about to say something else, but suddenly his mother was standing in front of them. "Let's go, Jake. We got to see about your pa."

"Bye, Sophie."

"Bye, Jake. And thanks."

✂

When the taxi pulled up at Mount Sinai Hospital, Sophie gazed in awe at the cream-colored, two-story building with its wrought-iron railings and lofty windows. Inside, they waited for over an hour before the doctor examined Mama and told her she had broken her ankle. But he decided to keep her in hospital for a few days to find out why she was having stomach pains.

"I knew it!" Mama said as the nurse helped her into bed. "I knew this would be the end of me! Next stop, the *feld*, the cemetery!"

"Shh, Mama, don't talk like that." Sophie leaned with her back against the wall. "They want to find out what's wrong with you, and then you'll be home again."

"And what about my poor Rose? Who will find out what happened to her?" Mama whimpered. "If Papa was here..." She got a faraway look in her eyes and started to cry. She groped for her handkerchief but there were no pockets in the drab hospital gown. Sophie gave Mama her handkerchief.

Sophie took her mother to Mount Sinai Hospital on
Yorkville Street because it was Jewish, provided kosher food,
and treated those who could not pay.

Mama wiped her eyes and blew her nose and tried to hand the soggy piece of cotton back, but Sophie shook her head. "Keep it. You need it more than me."

She turned to go. "You'll be fine, Mama," she said firmly. She knew she was trying to convince both of them. "I'll come see you after my picket duty tomorrow. As for Rose, I'll find out where this Mercer place is, and see what I can do. Leave it to me. Don't worry about it." She bent down to kiss her mother on the forehead. "And tomorrow, I'll bring a clean handkerchief."

That night was the first time Sophie had ever been alone in the flat. Although she heard the Bernsteins walking around above her on the third floor, and the Weinstocks on the first, everything was much too quiet. To her ears, even her own breathing seemed too noisy. The honking of a horn, the rustling of branches, someone shouting in the street—every noise startled her. She tried to read a library book for a while but couldn't concentrate on the words.

She thought she heard a sound close by, and opened the door to the summer kitchen. When Papa was still alive, he had lined the walls with shelves. He had magic hands, Mama used to say. He could make or fix anything.

Now Sophie gazed at the shelves where once there had been jars of jam, pickles, and sauerkraut. Overflowing bushel baskets of apples, carrots, and onions had rested on the floor, along with burlap bags that seemed to offer an endless supply of potatoes.

Now the shelves were almost empty; the baskets and bags held only a few soft, almost rotten vegetables.

Sophie closed the door, checked twice that it was locked, and went to bed. Her heart felt as empty as those burlap bags lying forlornly on the summer-kitchen floor.

What would she say to Jake—that is, if she ever saw him again? What would the doctor find was wrong with Mama? And what was happening to Rose at that Mercer jail? She lay shivering in bed for a long time before she finally fell asleep.

She dreamed that she was in a dark tunnel. The clammy walls narrowed around her as she walked. She tripped on loose cobblestones and almost fell down. She heard footsteps following her, getting closer. Someone crept up behind her and wrapped his thin fingers around her throat. He began to choke her. She couldn't breathe. She couldn't *move*—

She woke up coughing, her body tangled in the sheets. A faint light seeped in through the cracked window blind. She staggered to the window and struggled until she managed to open it partway and put a stick under it.

Cold air rushed in and she gulped it greedily. It was morning. She had to face another day. But this time, she would have to do it all alone.

CHAPTER 8
Keep Your Head Down

After leaving the Claremont station, the police car sped along King Street, crossed the railway tracks, and passed through a wrought-iron gate set in a high brick wall. A gravel driveway led to a huge brick building that looked like a fortress or a castle, complete with a steeple and turrets. Small, iron-barred windows stretched up and away as far as Rose could see. She shuddered and felt her stomach clench in fear.

The policeman unlocked the door, gripped Rose's arm, and yanked her out of the car. He led her up the stone steps and through an archway, and rang a bell on the heavy wooden door.

The sound reverberated in Rose's body. She felt as if she were growing smaller, like Alice, who swallowed the "Drink Me" potion so that she could open the little door and enter

Wonderland. But Rose knew deep in her bones that this was one door she did not want to pass through.

Almost immediately, a woman opened the door. She had blonde wavy hair and wore a navy-blue dress with a white collar. She didn't look at Rose, only at the policeman. Rose felt like an object, a piece of baggage transferred from one place to another.

She stood in the entrance hall, staring at nothing, thinking nothing, while the policeman and the woman exchanged some papers. The hall was cavernous, with nothing to break the space—not a chair or a bench; not even the ticking of a clock. It smelled of bleach and wax and something else Rose couldn't put her finger on. She suspected it was despair. She wished she could sit down, for she felt queasy and lightheaded. She leaned against the wall for support.

When he and the woman were done with the paperwork, the policeman hurried away without a backward glance. The woman led Rose down a long hallway to a room and held the door open. "I'm Mrs. Clark, the matron here," she said. "Go in and get changed. And make it snappy!" She pointed to a bench on one side of the room. "Your prison clothes are there. Put your other clothes in the paper bag with your name on it. Now move!"

She turned abruptly and left. Rose heard the door click shut behind her, and the sound echoed in her ears.

She changed into underwear, a long-sleeved woolen dress, a gray sweater that smelled of mothballs, long dark stockings, and black shoes. Everything was too big for her, but she knew she had no choice. She would have to follow orders here, without comment or question. Every time she put one of her own garments into the paper bag, it was as if she were losing part of herself.

After a few minutes, Mrs. Clark opened the door. She stood in the doorway, her arms crossed, a scowl on her face. "Follow me. And no talking."

She led Rose up two flights of stairs, along a corridor, and toward the entrance to what would be her section in the jail. While they walked, the clinking of the matron's keys jangled Rose's frayed nerves. She wrinkled her nose. The smell of bleach was stronger here.

Mrs. Clark unlocked a door and they entered a wide hallway with some twenty cells along one side. They walked down the hall until the matron halted abruptly and pointed to an empty cell. "Your home away from home," she said sarcastically.

Rose walked in and the iron door clanged shut behind her. Mrs. Clark walked away, the sound of her keys echoing along the long, empty corridor.

The room was tiny, with brick walls on three sides. A bare bulb screwed into the ceiling shed a stark light upon a narrow cot on which lay a thin cotton mattress, two sheets, a rough gray blanket, a pillow, and a pillowcase. Fastened to the wall was a small porcelain sink with one tap. In a container next to it were a bar of soap, a toothbrush, and a tin of tooth powder. A covered white toilet sat in the corner on the floor. A gray towel that might once have been white and a roll of toilet paper were on a chair next to the cot.

Rose shivered in the cool air and wished she still had her

coat. It was in the paper bag now, probably stuffed in some cubbyhole somewhere. Her body felt bent and frail, like one of the women she'd seen at the Old Folks' Home on Cecil Street. She looked around for insects—roaches, maybe, and spiders—but didn't see any. She shuddered.

She made the bed and lay down, too exhausted to think or feel. She felt broken. For the rest of the night she lay on the hard cot, cold, scared, alone.

Rose served her sentence in the Mercer Reformatory for Women, a huge forbidding-looking building with barred windows.

✂

The next morning, a loud bell woke Rose up. Mrs. Clark walked along the hallway, ringing the bell and calling, "Six-thirty. Wake up! Get dressed!"

The bell reminded Rose of the one her teachers had rung at Lansdowne Public School when recess was over. Her throat tightened at the memory. She wished she were a schoolgirl again, innocent and free, with only her studies to think about. She wished Papa were still alive; that Mama was well and happy; that she still had her dreams and ambitions. Was she really here, in prison? She covered her ears against the clanging of the bell and huddled under the scratchy blanket, squeezing her eyes shut and trying to imagine that she was home again.

At the sound of a second bell thirty minutes later, Mrs. Clark shouted, "Out! Everyone out!"

Rose huddled deeper under the blanket, but the matron burst into her cell and yanked the blanket off. The cold air was like an icy hand around her throat.

"I said *get up*," Mrs. Clark hissed. She smacked Rose on the head. "And make it snappy!"

Rose's head was ringing as she scrambled out of bed. With shaking fingers she slipped into her shoes, straightened the clothes she had slept in, and ran a comb through her tangled hair. She had only enough time to pee in the toilet and wash her hands before she stepped out of her cell and joined the other prisoners in the line for breakfast. She had the feeling they would be lining up a lot in this place.

"No talking!" Mrs. Clark ordered.

Rose followed the others to the mess hall downstairs. Women guards stood watching as the inmates sat down at their places, and told the new arrivals where to sit. Rose breathed a sigh of relief when she was allowed to go to Becky's table. She sat down next to her and hugged her. She had been worrying about what had happened to Becky ever since they had been separated at the police station.

A guard pushed them apart. "We'll have none of that," she said. "No physical contact. And quiet talking only."

Bread and milk were on the tables; a few older inmates plopped gray, mushy oatmeal porridge into their bowls. Rose would have eaten anything, she was so hungry. She gulped the black tea, grateful for the hot liquid as it slid down her throat.

"How are you doing?" Becky whispered.

Rose shrugged. "Not bad, I guess." She kept her eyes down. She wished she were invisible.

Becky sighed. "Thank God it's only for thirty days."

"You got thirty days too?"

Becky nodded.

Two other women were sitting at their table. One of them whispered, "You're new here, eh?" She raised her eyebrows and stared at them. "Name's Liz." The woman had pale skin, blonde straight hair, and light blue eyes. She reminded Rose of a movie star.

She remembered going to the movies for her fourteenth birthday. Mama hadn't wanted to spend the twenty-five cents but Papa had said, "How often does she turn fourteen?" They saw *The Broadway Melody*, and Rose loved the singing and dancing. (Mama said girls shouldn't show their bare legs like that, but Papa only smiled.) There won't be any singing or dancing here in prison, Rose thought.

She pushed away the memory and said, "I'm Rose and this is my friend, Becky."

"I'm Susan," whispered the woman sitting across from Rose. She had red frizzy hair and freckles. She seemed older than Liz, and her eyes darted around nervously. "But keep your voices down or we'll all get into trouble."

"Where do you live?" Liz asked.

Rose put a spoonful of oatmeal in her mouth. It was lumpy but it was warm and solid and comforting. "Near Kensington Market."

Susan said, "It's Cabbagetown for me."

Liz glanced at the guards. "Me, I live all over the place. When I'm not here."

"What're you in for?" Susan shoveled porridge into her mouth. "You seem like decent girls."

"We were on the picket line. The dressmakers' strike, you know."

"We got into an argument with some strike-breakers." Becky sipped her tea. "We were charged with vagrancy, but I don't know why. We have a home. We have families. It's not like we live on the street."

Susan snorted. "Vagrancy is what they charge you with if they don't know what else to do." She lowered her voice. "Or sometimes it's because we've broken the stupid liquor laws."

Liz chuckled. "Susan's been here the most. She's the veteran."

"Why?" asked Becky.

Susan shrugged. "Nothing serious. I was charged with being drunk and disorderly. That magistrate, Cohen's his name, he's got it in for me."

Liz took a hard look at Rose and Becky. "You Jews, like him?"

Rose felt her face getting red. She looked down at her feet. But Becky raised her chin. "Yeah, we're Jewish."

"So you must be rich," Liz said.

Rose shook her head. "Fat chance!"

Liz held up her hands. "Don't take it the wrong way. I didn't mean nothing bad by it."

Susan glanced at the guards standing near the door. "The first time I was arrested, Cohen fined me $13.25 or thirty days in jail. I couldn't scrape the fine together so I came here. After that, the cops kept arresting me. They charged me with incorrigibility—whatever that is."

"It's—" Rose began.

"Hush," Becky whispered. "Let her talk."

"Cohen kept giving me longer and longer jail terms. This time, I'm in for six months."

Rose gasped.

Susan twisted her mouth into what might have been a smile. One of her front teeth was missing. "Hell. It's okay. I've got a clean bed and three square meals a day."

"With the work they give you," Liz said, "time passes pretty fast."

Rose doubted that her time here would pass quickly enough.

CHAPTER 9

No Ifs, Ands, or Buts

In spite of her miserable night, Sophie was on the picket line on Tuesday morning. She had never felt so cold in her life. The freezing north wind cut through her coat and made her bones ache. Her socks felt like soggy sponges inside her worn-out boots. Her fingers were numb in her thin gloves. Her arms and shoulders hurt from holding up her sign, WE WANT A LIVING WAGE!

It was just their luck that they were striking during the worst snowfall in fifty-five years. Unemployed men had been hired to shovel the snow, while trucks hauled their loads away. People said it would take four days to clear all the snow.

The businesses on Spadina had slowed to a crawl. A lot of workers were on strike and had no money to buy food or other necessities. Chickens and ducks were squawking in their wooden crates; carp and whitefish were swimming in their tanks; people were marching on empty stomachs.

Every day on the walk to strike duty, Sophie passed Lansdowne Public School. She stopped to watch the kids playing in the schoolyard, or gazed at the windows decorated with cutout paper snowflakes. Soon the snowflakes would be replaced by green shamrocks and figures of leprechauns hiding a pot of gold. It all made her feel much older than her fourteen years.

This was the view of Spadina Avenue from an upper floor window of the Darling Building.

The newspaper reporters had already lost interest in the strike, distracted by other news, like the construction of the grand Canada Life building or the increasing number of car crashes on city streets. The news about the strike had been shoved to the inside of the paper, on page three. Probably by next week, Sophie thought, we'll be on the back page. Bernard Shane and the other union leaders tried to encourage the strikers with speeches about standing strong, but she heard the picketers muttering among themselves.

"It's been two weeks, but it feels like twenty."

"We can't hold up against the owners—they're too rich."

"Where's the help Shane and the rest of them promised us?"

Sophie went to the hospital that evening, but Mama was asleep. "We're still waiting for the results of the tests," the nurse said.

Sophie felt that her life was on hold—waiting for Mama to come home, waiting for Rose to get out of jail, waiting for the strike to be over.

On her way home, she met Mary, one of the girls who worked with her at the factory.

"Sophie? Where were you after the trouble on Friday? Someone told me you were knocked down by a horse."

"I'm all right. I—"

"We're going to keep picketing until Mr. Fox gives in to our demands."

Sophie shook her head. "Mr. Fox isn't giving in, though

a lot of other firms have already signed contracts with their workers."

Mary tsked. "So what? More than half of us are still out on strike. We have to keep going until *all* the bosses recognize the union. Otherwise, the contracts won't be worth a red cent. The bosses will sign them, get the workers back, and then just ignore the agreements."

"But my sister was arrested and my mother is in hospital—"

"No exceptions! We've all got our troubles."

"But—"

"No buts. I'll see you on the picket line tomorrow."

"Yeah. See you."

Sophie's life was turning out to be exceptional, but not in the way she'd hoped. She had dreamed of becoming a high school English teacher, and she still loved to read whenever she had a chance.

She read books in both Yiddish and English. Among her favorites were the Sholem Aleichem stories that Papa had loved. Whenever she felt worried or troubled, she read Aleichem's stories about Tevye the Dairyman in the Russian village of Boyberik. Her spirits would lift up immediately. After all, she thought, if Tevye could stay hopeful in spite of all his sorrows, then she could too.

But lately, Sophie had had no time to read or think or dream. Sometimes she felt that she was sinking in quicksand, and that she would never get out.

✂

After Sophie finished picket duty on Wednesday, she went to visit Mama at the hospital again. She had to hurry because visiting hours were short, and she wanted to walk to save the streetcar fare. In some places she had to climb over piles of snow. The socks inside her boots got soaked and the wind kept blowing her hat off. Her fingers felt numb. If only she could just go home, and find Mama and Rose there!

After almost an hour she reached the hospital. She found Mama sitting up in bed, a mountain of pillows behind her back. Three other women shared the room. One was moaning and thrashing about; another was asleep, snoring loudly; the third was yakking a mile a minute to a skinny man who must have been her henpecked husband.

In spite of the disturbances and the short cast on her leg, Mama hadn't looked so good in a long time.

"Sophie!" she said, reaching out her hand. "I'm glad to see you. I've been alone all day." She waved at the other patients. "Except for my fellow prisoners. Which reminds me"—she lowered her voice—"have you gone to see Rose?"

"Not yet, Mama. I will, as soon as I have a chance." She squeezed her mother's hand. "How are you feeling?"

"Not bad. As they say, 'If you're healthy, you're wealthy.'" She leaned toward Sophie. "But the nurses aren't polite to me."

"What do you mean?" Sophie looked around for a chair, but the henpecked husband was sitting on the only one. Her feet and legs were wet and cold and she shivered in spite of the heat coming from the radiator. She sat down gingerly on the edge of the bed.

"They always want I should be on their schedule," Mama said. "They should better be on *mine!*"

Sophie heard the buzz of voices from the hallway. "But they're busy, Mama. They have to run this hospital efficiently."

"Humph! If they listened to me, they could learn a thing or two." Mama squirmed and tried to move her leg but grimaced with pain. "*Shepseleh*, my lamb, rub my shoulders a little. So much lying in bed is making me stiff. Soon I'll be good for nothing!"

Sophie rubbed her shoulders, but after a few minutes Mama pulled away. "Open the drawer." She pointed to the bedside table. "In there is a piece of paper."

Sophie opened the drawer and handed her mother a long sheet of paper.

"And the pencil too."

Mama took the pencil, licked the lead, and started writing furiously. "Passover is coming soon and we have a lot of work to do."

"Passover?" Sophie said. Her favorite holiday, and she had completely forgotten about it!

"Of course Passover!" Mama waved the paper in Sophie's face. "I'll be home soon, but you need to do a few things before I come home."

"Yes, Mama," Sophie sighed. Do a few things, and be on the picket line, and come to see Mama, and go to visit Rose. Forget about reading any books!

For the next half-hour, Mama wrote her list, detailing all the work Sophie had to do before her mother got home. "We don't have too much time to prepare, and you must help me now that Rose…isn't home."

"But Mama, the strike—"

Mama waved her protestations away. "Strikes come and strikes go. But our people have been celebrating Passover for hundreds, for thousands of years. And we'll still be celebrating Passover long after the strike is finished."

"I know, but—"

"No buts! You will go home and do what I say." Mama had a wistful look on her face. "And if we're lucky, our Rose will be home for Passover."

"But Mama," Sophie said, "she has to stay there…in that place"—Sophie couldn't bring herself to say jail—"for thirty days. Passover will be over by then. At least, the *seders* will."

Mama shook her head. "If God could force Pharaoh to free the Jewish people from Egypt, He can free our Rose from jail."

"But Mama—"

"No more buts." She sank back into her pillows. "Now be a good girl and do what I say."

Just then, a young woman brought Mama's supper and placed it on the table. The smell of food made Sophie's mouth water. She hadn't eaten all day, and she felt so weak that she was afraid she'd faint if she stayed. On the other hand, if a person is going to faint, the hospital is a good place to do it. Even better than a police station.

Mama looked sharply at her daughter. "When was the last time you ate?"

Sophie shrugged. "I can't remember."

Mama wagged her finger. "You'll share with me."

Sophie began to shake her head but Mama said, "No ifs, ands, or buts. You have to eat to keep up your strength!"

"And you?"

"Me? I feel as strong as a horse!"

So Sophie sat beside Mama on the bed and shared her supper: half the meatloaf, half the potatoes, half the canned peas, and half the applesauce. She felt guilty and hoped the other patients didn't notice, but Mama said, "If you don't eat with me, *I* won't eat."

So what could Sophie do? She ate half of Mama's supper, and was grateful for it.

CHAPTER 10
Let Her People Go

On Sunday, Sophie went down the list that Mama had given her: She washed the cupboards and put new paper on the shelves. She cleaned the icebox and scrubbed the stove. She washed all the windows and floors.

While she worked, she wondered why Jake got so mad at her when she said he didn't understand. Why did she feel she had to defend herself?

She wondered why he wasn't in school any longer. Why he had to sell papers on the corner.

She stopped scrubbing the sink, the water dripping from the cloth. Maybe *she* was the one who didn't understand. Maybe she was the one who wasn't being fair. She shook her head and wrung out the cloth. One thing was sure. If she saw Jake again, she would apologize for what she had said.

When she had finished the housework, Sophie made herself a peanut butter sandwich and sat down at the table. She had always liked the table, with its sturdy wooden legs and metal top. When she and Rose were little, they used to play on it and not worry they'd wreck it. Mama used to roll out her strudel dough on the tabletop. She'd spread jam on the dough, add cocoa and sugar, and sprinkle it with raisins. Then she'd roll it up and bake it in the oven.

Mama would do her mending at the table, or the girls would play dominoes or checkers. Papa would read the Yiddish newspaper aloud as Mama finished cooking.

But Sophie's favorite thing about the table was the small drawer on one of its longer sides. It was the family's "junk" drawer, in which you could find any number of things: pencil stubs, elastic bands, old receipts, pieces of string, odd buttons, or a pack of cards.

Jake didn't want to talk to Sophie again, especially after their last conversation. Every time he thought about it, he felt his blood boil. He wasn't Jewish, but that didn't make him some kind of alien from outer space! But he couldn't stop thinking about her. There was something about Sophie that drew him, almost against his will.

The next time Jake saw Sophie among the picketers in front of the Balfour Building, he went up to her and tapped her on the shoulder.

She looked startled and almost dropped her sign. "What? What do you want?"

Jake almost walked away then, but he gathered his courage. "Sorry I startled you." He took off his cap and twisted it in his hands. "Can I talk to you?"

Sophie looked at the other strikers, holding their signs and plodding along the slushy sidewalk. At first, Jake could see she didn't want to talk, but then she got a kind of lost look in her eyes.

"All right." Sophie stuck out her chin. Already Jake knew that was a sign that she'd made a decision about something. "When?"

"When do you finish picket duty?"

"In a couple of hours. At five o'clock."

Jake made some quick calculations in his head. He had to sell his newspapers or his family wouldn't have enough to eat that night. "Can I meet you at six?"

She hesitated and then nodded. "All right. I'll wait for you at United Bakers." She smiled shyly. "Mama said I'm not eating enough. She gave me ten cents."

Jake put his cap back on his head. "I know where it is. I'll meet you there." His heart was beating so loudly he thought everyone on Spadina Avenue could hear it.

✂

Jake paused at the door. The delicious smell of warm bagels was overpowering. His mouth began to water.

He let out his breath when he saw Sophie in the crowded restaurant. He was glad she'd found a table, instead of sitting at the counter. He didn't want any nosey parkers listening to them talk. When he reached her table, he cleared his throat. "Hi."

She looked up. "Hi." A half-eaten egg salad sandwich was on her plate. She pointed to a chair opposite. Jake took his cap off and sat down.

A waitress came up to the table. She wore a black blouse and skirt and white apron. She placed two glasses of water on the table and then tapped her pencil on the pad. "What'll you have?"

Jake hesitated, thinking of the money in his pocket; thinking that he shouldn't be spending it in a restaurant. He swallowed hard. "A bagel?" He knew it was the cheapest item on the menu.

Staff take a break outside United Bakers, a popular restaurant. Jake and Sophie met there, hoping they could talk in private.

"What kind? We got poppy seed or sesame or plain."

"Sesame."

"Plain or toasted?"

"Toasted. And a coffee please." Jake looked at Sophie. "Do you want anything else?"

Sophie shook her head. "No. Thanks."

"Fine. Be back in a jiffy." The waitress hurried to the next table.

Sophie picked up her sandwich and put it down again. She crossed her arms and stared at Jake. "What did you want to talk about?"

Now that Jake was finally face to face with Sophie, he didn't know what to say. He took a napkin from the holder and started shredding it into tiny pieces. It was hard to look at her.

"Jake—"

"Sophie—" They both laughed.

"Ladies first."

"I'm sorry I acted like that the other day." Sophie blushed. "I didn't mean what I said."

"Maybe you were right." The napkin was turning into confetti. "Maybe we *are* from two different worlds." Jake gulped some water and put the glass down. His hand was shaking. "I don't really understand. But I *want* to!"

She leaned forward and touched his hand. He felt his face redden. "Let's get to know each other better." She looked around the crowded restaurant filled with workers—mostly Jewish. She had an uneasy feeling in the pit of her stomach, but she tried to ignore the feeling. "Maybe we have more in common than you think."

"Here's your order." The waitress plopped down the bagel and coffee.

For the next hour, they talked about many things: about the dressmakers' strike; about what was happening in the world, like the Empire State Building in New York City, which was almost finished; about Charlie Chaplin's new movie, *City Lights*; about their families; about their hopes and dreams.

All the while, Jake nibbled on the bagel to make it last as long as possible. People were standing in line for a table, but Jake didn't care. He could have talked with Sophie all night long.

Finally, the waitress placed the bill on the table. "I'm sorry. You gotta leave now. Other customers are waiting to sit down and this is our busy time."

The shock of cold air hit them as they walked out of the restaurant. Jake put his cap on and hugged his arms to his chest. "Sophie, can I see you again?"

Sophie hesitated. She knew Mama and Rose would have a fit if they knew she was seeing a non-Jewish boy. She nodded.

Right there, on the crowded sidewalk, Jake leaned over and kissed Sophie on the cheek. All the way home, his gentle kiss kept Sophie warm.

CHAPTER 11

Dear Rose, I Don't Know What to Say...

On Tuesday, Sophie knocked on the door of the doctor's small, cluttered office. Dr. Levine was engrossed in a pile of papers but looked up as she entered the room. He was a middle-aged man with a balding head and glasses. "Yes?"

"Doctor, I'm Sophie Abramson, Mrs. Abramson's daughter."

Dr. Levine waved Sophie over to the wooden chair across from his desk. "How can I help you?"

She held onto the back of the chair, then made her way around it, and sat down. She straightened her back. "Doctor, what's wrong with my mother?"

The doctor considered her. "You're rather young to be asking, aren't you? How old are you?" He looked over her shoulder, as if expecting someone else to come through the door.

"I'm fourteen," Sophie said. "And there's no one else. At least, not right now." She hesitated. "Papa died over a year ago and my sister—"

Dr. Levine held up his hand. His fingers were slender and his fingernails were immaculate. "Everyone has a sad story nowadays. It's these hard times and—"

"I know." Sophie's shoulders sagged. "We...we dressmakers are on strike."

He raised his eyebrows. "I read in the *Daily Star* that the strike isn't going so well."

Sophie shrugged. "A little bit of good, a little bit of bad."

He smiled kindly and searched through his papers. "Let me tell you about your mother."

"Yes, please."

"She has a peptic ulcer in her stomach, probably caused by stress." He looked up. "Is she worried about something?"

"Who isn't, nowadays?"

"Hmm. Or maybe she's been eating the wrong kind of food?"

"Is that why she's been complaining of stomach pains? And why she has no appetite and she's losing weight?"

"Probably." Dr. Levine asked Sophie a few questions about Mama's diet and daily habits, and then stood up. "Let's go see her. I have some things I need to say to her."

Sophie followed Dr. Levine down the corridor to Mama's room, where he wasted no time getting to the point. "Now, Mrs. Abramson, what's this I hear about you eating fried foods and not getting any exercise?"

Mama tried to raise herself up on the bed. She smoothed her hair with her hand and looked accusingly at Sophie.

"Mrs. Abramson, I want you to listen carefully."

Mama nodded and sank back against the pillows. "Yes, doctor."

He sat down on a chair beside the bed. "I'm sorry to tell you, but you have a peptic ulcer."

Mama put her hand to her chest. "An ulcer! Oy vey! My friend Bessie had one and she—"

Dr. Levine smiled. "Now look. You're not your friend Bessie. So far, it's just a *small* ulcer. The last thing I want to do is operate and remove half your stomach."

"Half…my stomach?" Mama bit her lip.

"You can go home now," he told her, "but come back to see me in three months. In the meantime, you are not allowed to drink coffee or tea, or eat fried or spicy food."

"No fried onions with scrambled eggs?"

"No."

"No fried liver?"

He shook his head. "Only baked liver."

Mama made a face. "Not even a blintz?"

"Not even the *thought* of a blintz!"

"Maybe a *latke*, a potato pancake? Or a glass of tea?"

Dr. Levine looked at her severely. "You want to get better? And not have an operation?"

"Yes, doctor. I mean, no doctor."

"Then follow my orders." He glanced at Sophie. "And, young lady, I expect you to help your mother." He leaned over and whispered in Sophie's ear. "Watch her like a hawk!"

✂

They took a taxi home, with Mama complaining all the way about the money it cost.

Sophie eased her onto the couch in the front room. "Keep your foot up, Mama."

"Yes, doctor."

"I have to go to the drugstore to buy you some antacid. Will you be all right?"

Mama waved her away. "Of course I'll be all right." She reached over and opened her purse. "Take my change purse. Don't pay too much. Get a small bottle."

At Koffler's Drugstore on College Street, she found the medicine and stood in line at the cash register. She recognized a few of the people sitting on stools at the lunch counter, warming their chapped hands around cups of coffee. Most people couldn't afford more than toast and coffee, but they tried to make it last as long as possible.

Ben, the son of Herman the Cutter, was sitting at the counter and waved her over when she was about to leave. "How's your mother?" He had brown curly hair, brown eyes, and a slender nose. She thought that he was quite handsome and felt herself blush.

"Your mother?" Ben repeated.

"Oh. Sorry. I guess I have a lot on my mind."

Ben leaned over and lowered his voice. "Don't we all?" He looked at Sophie with kind eyes. "And Rose? Have you seen her? How's she doing?"

Sophie shook her head. "They wouldn't let me in. They said I was too young. But I'm going to write her a letter."

"When you do, will you give her my regards?"

"I will." Sophie turned to leave, but Ben touched her on the arm.

"Wait! Tell her…that I admire what she's done and, you know, that I miss her. I really miss her."

Sophie nodded. "You can tell her yourself when she comes out."

Ben smiled. "I will. I will definitely do that."

When Sophie walked into the flat, Mama said, "I've been thinking…"

"About?"

"About both the seders. How can I prepare a seder in my condition?"

"Stop worrying," Sophie said. "The Weinstocks downstairs invited us to come to their flat for the first one."

"And for the second? I've never in my life missed a seder." She sighed as if it were the end of the world.

"The landsmanshaft, our benefit society, has rented a hall on Cecil Street for a communal seder," Sophie said. "We'll go there."

Mama slumped down into the worn sofa. "It won't be like the old days."

Sophie knew what she meant. With Papa dead and Rose in jail, their family had shrunk to almost nothing. "At least you won't have to do all the cooking. That's a good thing, isn't it?"

Mama looked at her strangely. "But cooking and baking is something I know how to do. How can I just sit here like a bump on a log, doing nothing?" She snorted. "As they say, 'The hardest work is to be idle.'"

She sat up straighter and her face brightened. "You know, when I was in the hospital, I saw some women cooking there. Kosher cooking, but it wasn't very tasty."

"So? What do you expect from hospital food?"

"What do I expect? It should be better! When I get my cast off, I'll go there." She pressed her lips together and her eyes were shining. "I'll ask them for a job as a cook. Me, I never open a can. I make a good meal. An expert like me, they'll hire in a snap."

"If you want a reference, just ask me. I love your cooking! Especially your blintzes and *kreplach* and chicken soup and—"

"Stop! Stop!" Mama laughed. "So many compliments, I'll get a swelled head." She paused. "Now, let's have a nice glass of tea."

"Mama, you know what the doctor said—"

"Oy! No tea." She sighed. "All right, okay. A glass of hot water with some milk."

"That I'll get for you. And Mama?"

"What?"

"I didn't have enough money to buy matzos, but the Ladies' Montefiore Society from Holy Blossom, the fancy synagogue on Bond Street, gave us eggs and matzos and other things we'll need for the holiday."

Mama eyed the cardboard box on the kitchen table. "I hate taking charity!"

Sophie began to take the items out of the box and put them in the cupboard. "We can't get by on the measly strike pay from the union."

"I know, but when will it end?"

"I wish I knew."

✂

Later that night, Sophie opened the little drawer in the kitchen table and took out a pad of paper and a pencil. She began to write a letter.

Dear Rose,

I don't know what to say, but I guess you're wondering what's happening with us. I tried to visit you but they wouldn't let me in. (They said I was too young.)

Mama and I went to the police station the Monday after you were arrested to look for you. We found out you'd been taken to the Mercer Reformatory (shiver). How are you doing there? Do you get enough to eat? Are you warm and safe? (I sound like Mama now!)

When we were leaving the station, Mama slipped on the icy steps and fell down. I took her to the Mount Sinai Hospital—you can imagine how much she *kvetched* about going—and the doctor said she'd broken her ankle. On top of that, he kept her there for a few days because of her stomach pains and it turns out she has an ulcer. She's got to avoid all the foods she likes—fried onions and potatoes, *schmaltz*, and all the rest. She didn't like to hear that one bit!

Today I brought her home from the hospital. Before that, I was cleaning the flat like a *meshuggeneh*, a crazy woman (Mama's orders!), to get it ready for Passover. You know, I never realized how much work it is. Now I've got dishpan hands (ugh).

I wish you could come home for Passover, but I guess that's impossible.

Some of us are still on strike and I have picket duty every day. Not on Saturday or Sunday. (I get time off for good behavior. Papa's joke!) To tell you the truth, I don't want to go on picket duty anymore. Things are getting rough and I'm starting to get scared. I wish you were home. I need my older (wiser) sister right about now.

Strikers and scabs, the strike-breakers, keep fighting outside the factories. Some of the firms have hired "private detectives" to protect the scabs when they go in to work. The detectives are nothing but gangsters and thugs who beat up innocent people for no reason. They shove us around, step on our feet, and kick us in the shins. The police stand by and give us no help. The government does nothing.

In the last few days, while Mama was in the hospital, I was alone in the flat. I hated it! But I shouldn't complain so much. Being in jail must be a thousand times worse.

I'm sorry this letter is so full of negative things. Yesterday I saw my first robin and the crocuses are coming out. Things have to get better. They just HAVE to!

I miss you a lot. Please come home soon. (And I won't ever complain again about sharing the bed with you!)

Your loving sister,
Sophie

P.S. Guess who I saw at the drugstore? Ben! He asked about you and says he admires you. (I think he has a crush on you.)

CHAPTER 12
A Shame and a Disgrace

When Sophie came home from picket duty three weeks later, Rose was slumped on the couch. Mama was sitting beside her but neither one spoke.

"Rose!"

Rose looked startled, even scared. Then her body crumpled and she began rocking back and forth as if no one else were there.

Sophie walked over to her and squatted in front of her.

"I've been trying to ask her," Mama said. "What happened? Why didn't she answer our letters?"

"I knew your thirty days were up," Sophie said, "but I didn't know exactly when you'd be home. Why didn't you let us know?"

Rose stared at the floor and mumbled, "You didn't visit me." She spoke so softly that Sophie had trouble hearing her. "I was desperate for you to come." She looked at Sophie with a look that made Sophie cringe. "Why didn't you come?"

Sophie put her hand on Rose's arm but Rose shook it off as if her sister were a louse crawling on her skin. "I told you in my letter, I wanted to but they said I wasn't old enough. I had to be sixteen. And Mama was sick and hurt and—"

"What letter? I didn't get any letters." Rose stood up and stomped out of the front room. They heard the door to Mama's bedroom close and then heard sobbing from behind the door.

"Go to her, *shepseleh*," Mama whispered. "I don't know what to say or do."

Rose thought they had it bad at Fox's factory, but it was a hundred times worse in prison. When the guard led the prisoners to the workshop, she couldn't believe her eyes. The sewing machines looked like antiques—so old that even Mr. Fox wouldn't have used them. The prisoners had to sew with those ancient machines eight hours a day, six days a week. The bobbin and thread kept bunching up and getting tangled. Rose had to stop all the time to fix one thing or another.

She had been proud of the work she did at the factory, but now everything turned out a mess. The workshop was cold and damp, and the light was so poor that sewing gave her a headache. But the bugs were the worst, especially the cockroaches. They would suddenly appear on the fabric, even on her hands, and then skitter away. One day she found a spider in her porridge, and shoved the bowl away. She kept thinking of how the garment workers had gone on strike for better wages. Here at the Mercer, they paid the prisoners five cents a day. She wondered why they even bothered.

Rose had been at the Mercer for eight days when she reached the point where she couldn't stand it anymore. Her machine had stalled for the third time that morning; the thread in the bobbin kept breaking. But worst of all was the supervisor, a middle-aged woman named Louise, who leaned over her while she tried to work.

Louise would pretend to show her how to do something, but then her hand would "accidentally" touch Rose. At first she touched her shoulder or back. But that morning Louise touched Rose's breast. "Don't do that," Rose hissed and shoved Louise's hand aside.

Louise leaned heavily against Rose. "Are you sure you want to act like that?" She whispered in Rose's ear with her sour breath, "I can make it easier for you here. A pretty girl like you…"

"What do you mean?" Rose's voice shook.

"Come into my office at lunch break and…I'll explain."

"Leave me alone." Rose tried to focus on the needle going through the cloth. But a few minutes later, two husky guards yanked her up by her arms and led her away. They dragged her down to the basement, along a clammy corridor, and dumped her inside a detention cell. She had to brace her arms against the cold walls so she didn't fall down. She heard the loud click of the metal lock behind her.

"Let me out of here!" Rose pounded on the steel door. "What did I do?"

"Insubordination," one of the guards jeered. "Three days in solitary."

Gradually, Rose got used to the dimness of the cell. The low-watt light bulb on the ceiling was always on and seemed to pierce the space behind her eyes no matter how tightly she squeezed them shut.

Rose felt bombarded by noises she couldn't decipher—snatches of conversation, feet walking above her cell, doors opening and clanging shut, whistles blowing at night. Worst of all were the little rustlings that made her jumpy—bugs, bugs everywhere.

The cell was seven feet by thirteen feet—she counted every inch—as she paced back and forth, back and forth. After a while she didn't even do that. She had nothing to do and no one to talk to, except for the guards who visited her three times a day with her meals. But their silent visits terrified her and she withdrew into her shell more with every passing day.

She lay on the cot and had strange waking thoughts. Papa was talking to her, telling her how disappointed he was; Mama was bringing her some chicken soup but the bowl had holes in it, and when she tried to feed Rose, the bowl was empty; Sophie was laughing at her and saying, "I knew you'd get into trouble! Now I'm the only child and I *like* it!"

She imagined Ben shaking his head, saying sadly, "How can I go out with a girl like you? A girl who's been in jail? I wanted to be your boyfriend, but now it's *a harpeh un a shandeh*, a shame and a disgrace."

She imagined all their mocking faces appearing and disappearing on the cold brick walls. She pressed her hands to her ears and shut her eyes tightly but it did no good. The voices and faces haunted every waking moment and pressed into her dreams, crushing her spirit and her will. She felt as if the darkness was going deep inside her.

By the time they let her out after three days of solitary confinement, she thought she was going crazy.

The day she returned to the prisoners' workshop, Louise sidled up to her. "Enjoy your time away?" she whispered. Her hand was on Rose's shoulder, digging into it with her long fingernails.

Rose didn't answer but kept her head down. She wished, she prayed, she could be invisible.

Louise pressed harder. "You get yourself cleaned up, and I'll see you in my office tomorrow at lunch break." She released her fingers and stroked Rose's back. "Stay on my good side, honey, and you'll be just fine."

For the rest of her time at the Mercer, Rose did whatever Louise wanted. Rose was her slave, her servant, her victim. The thought of going back to solitary terrified Rose so much that she would do anything to stay out of it.

Every day was worse than the one before. But Rose was counting the days until they would release her. That promise of escape was a straw she grasped with every fiber of her being.

When her thirty days were up and they let Rose out of the Mercer, she wasn't sure what to do or where to go. She wasn't sure she should go home. She knew her mind had fled to a strange place, and she didn't want to worry Mama or Sophie. But she didn't know where else to go.

Was the strike still on? She didn't know and, really, she didn't care. Where was the girl who had turned off the switch at the factory? Where was her courage? Where was her strong will? They were buried under the stone floors of her prison cell, or maybe behind the door of Louise's stifling office. Rose might go home, but part of her remained in the prison.

✂

Sophie knocked on the door. "Rose?"

Rose didn't answer.

"Rose?"

Rose couldn't answer.

Sophie rattled the doorknob. "Rose, unlock the door or I'll break it down!"

Rose dragged herself to the door, unlocked it, and crept back to bed.

Sophie walked into the room and sat down on the bed. "What's the matter? Why are you acting so strangely?"

Rose shrugged and turned to face the wall. She felt as if a black cloud were weighing her down, down, down through the mattress and onto the floor. But when Sophie put her hand on her shoulder, Rose jerked away. "Leave me alone!"

"What's happened to you?"

"Nothing. I just want to be alone." Her body stiffened. "Please go! Get out of here!"

Sophie's eyes filled with tears. "You're my sister. I love you. I want to help."

"There's nothing you can do for me. Now go away and leave me alone!"

While Sophie was out picketing with the strikers, Mama needed Rose, so Rose tried to help her. She managed to get dressed and pad around the house, but she never knew when the black cloud might come back, or how long it would last.

Sophie and Mama told her she was a hero of working people everywhere. Why did those words sound so hollow in her ears? They told her that Mr. Shane, the union organizer, had come to visit her. She didn't care. Mama was embarrassed to tell him that Rose wouldn't see him. They told her that Ethel and Sadie from the factory had baked a cake for her, but Rose could not eat even a small slice.

About a week after Rose had come home, Sophie tried talking to her again. She took her a bowl of soup. Rose propped herself up on the bed and stared at it. She hadn't had any appetite for a long time.

"Eat something," Sophie pleaded. "Mama told me how to make your favorite potato soup."

"With browned onions?"

Sophie nodded.

Rose picked up the spoon but it felt too heavy. She put it

down and shoved the bowl back at Sophie. Her mouth was dry and her stomach ached.

Sophie reached for the spoon. "Here, I'll help you."

Rose felt like a baby, but it was comforting to swallow the warm soup. She hadn't tasted anything so good in a long time.

"The strike will be over soon," Sophie said. "I wish the union would hurry up and settle with all the owners!"

"Me too."

"The firms that are holding out met with the union yesterday."

Rose took the spoon from Sophie. "What happened?"

Sophie shrugged. "The talks collapsed."

Rose swallowed another spoonful of soup.

"And I heard that one of the owners let ten strike-breakers sleep in his building."

"Why?"

"He was afraid that if they went home, they wouldn't be able to come back through the picket line."

"I bet that wasn't too comfortable."

"They had to sleep on a bunch of rags."

Rose couldn't help smiling. "I'd rather sleep in my own bed."

Sophie put her hand on her sister's arm. "I'm glad you're home, Rose."

Rose hesitated but then reached out and covered Sophie's hand with her own. "So am I." Then she frowned. "What happened the day I was arrested? You were knocked down, weren't you?"

Sophie put her hand to her head. "Oh that!" She shrugged. "My battle scar, I guess." She explained what had happened on the day Becky and Rose had been arrested.

"Are you okay now?"

Sophie's eyes filled with tears. "I'm better now that you're home. And guess what?" She smiled in a way Rose had never seen before.

"There's a boy…who likes me."

"You've been busy while I was in jail!"

Sophie giggled. "It just sort of happened." She told Rose about Jake, but she could see that Rose was not pleased to hear that Jake wasn't Jewish.

Then Sophie told Rose about the time she had met Ben at the drugstore, and how he had asked about her. It gave Rose a sick feeling in the pit of her stomach. Would she ever be able to have a boyfriend? Could she let a man touch her, after what Louise had done to her at the Mercer? The thought made her feel unclean, damaged. She had grown up quickly at the Mercer. She wasn't a child anymore.

Mama knocked on the door and opened it before they had a chance to say, "Come in." She limped over to the bed but tripped on the soup bowl Sophie had put on the floor. Both girls reached out and caught her before she fell down.

"Dishes all over the floor? You want I should break the other ankle?" But Rose could tell she was joking.

"Sorry," Sophie said.

Mama bent over and kissed Rose on the forehead. "*Lachtikeh*, my darling, I am glad you are finally home, but it is time to go to sleep already."

"Soon, Mama."

"Now, Rose."

"Okay. You're the boss."

CHAPTER 13
You Can't Eat Moral Support

It was the following Monday—April 13—and the strike had dragged into its eighth week. Although the weather was pleasant now, with warmer temperatures and light rain showers, it was getting harder and harder for people to stay on the picket line. Nobody was sure whether the workers were winning or losing.

At first, most of the strikers had been united. They would joke a bit, sing a song or two, and tease each other. They refused to give in, even though the bosses hired thugs to protect the strike-breakers; even though some of the picketers were getting hurt or arrested. But now the union had signed contracts with a number of factories, and many workers had gone back to their jobs.

Only six hundred strikers were left, of the fifteen hundred

who had started. Now they marched in silence, their mouths set and their feet heavy. They still argued with the strike-breakers when they crossed the picket line, but what else could they do? With the police and judges on the owners' side, the strikers felt more and more helpless.

Although Mama cooked filling food like porridge and potato soup, Sophie felt hungry all the time. Her stomach was constantly aching and she didn't have much energy. When she looked in the mirror, she almost didn't recognize herself. Her face was pale; her hair was limp like cooked noodles. She wished Mama would stop reminding them, "Poor people cook with a lot of water."

Rose was becoming more like her old self, but she still didn't want to go out much. Bernard Shane had asked her to go back on strike duty, but she had refused. No one pressed her. The spark seemed to have gone out of her, and no one knew what to say or do. Sophie felt she was tiptoeing around her sister all the time, but she kept trying to persuade her to get involved with other people.

When she asked Rose to come with her to the weekly union meeting at the Lyceum, Rose shook her head. "What's the use?"

"It's a lot of use! We have to show that we still care—that we're united against the owners!"

Rose raised her eyebrows. "It won't do any good. They've got all the power. We're like *shmatas* they use and throw away."

"Don't talk like that! What happened to your fight? You used to care about the union."

Rose avoided looking at Sophie. "I don't know. A lot has

happened since the strike began." She shrugged. "Why don't you be the agitator for both of us?"

"Please come with me to the meeting." Sophie nudged her. "Hey, maybe you'll see Ben there."

Rose looked at her and smiled. "Okay. You win. But give me a few minutes to get ready." Sophie waited impatiently as her sister washed her hands and face, brushed her teeth, and combed her hair. She even changed into her second-best dress.

They linked arms as they walked along Spadina Avenue. The days were getting longer, and Sophie basked in the warming rays of the setting sun. She breathed deeply, feeling that the chains of winter had loosened their hold at last.

The Lyceum hall smelled the same as last time—of sweat and stale cigarette smoke, of bleach and floor wax. Everyone ignored Sophie and crowded around Rose as if she were a Hollywood star.

"You're our hero!" Ethel said.

"What was it like in jail?" Herman the Cutter asked.

"Welcome back!" Sadie said.

Rose didn't move. Her face was expressionless, as if she were made of wood.

Sophie pushed through the crowd of well-wishers. "Excuse me. We need to find some chairs." She wanted to go up front, but Rose shook her head and pointed to two chairs near the back of the hall.

They sat down, and Rose closed her eyes and sighed. Sophie could see that it was still hard for her to be with people.

The scene was very different from the meeting when the

ILGWU had first voted to go on strike. Empty chairs were scattered around the hall. People moved about, restless, gazing at the clock on the wall. They were anxious to go home, to go to the coffee shop, to play cards—anything but sit in a drafty union hall listening to the same old speeches.

The workers who had already signed contracts didn't have the energy to go to union meetings now. They were in the busy season, working more than twelve hours a day. After work, a lot of the women had to go home and do housework and, for most of them, take care of children.

Sophie thought about those women and why they had voted for a strike in the first place. They had been so determined to win a workweek of forty-four hours. The women and girls had gone back to work, but found that the new contracts were not being honored and working conditions were just as bad as they had been before the strike.

Bernard Shane walked up to the podium. Sophie thought he looked older than the last time she had seen him. He had dark bags under his eyes. His shoulders were stooped, and he squinted at the papers he was holding. "Fellow workers," he began, "our strike has been a long one."

"You can say that again!" Sadie yelled as she stood up, holding onto the chair in front of her for support.

Shane lifted his hand but continued. "As you probably know, this week Mr. Monteith, the Ontario Minister of Labour, called a meeting between the union and the factory owners. He's been trying to settle the strike." He sighed. "To make a long story short, the employers refused to attend the meeting."

"What a surprise!" Morris the Presser shouted.

"Let him talk!" Herman shouted back.

"It's obvious that no one in the government can do a thing to end the strike." Shane smiled wryly. "I dream that one day there will be a law forcing the owners to agree to our demands."

"A *nechtiker tog!*" Morris the Presser called out. "Impossible!"

"Where's all the help you promised us?" Sadie's knuckles were white as she grasped the chair. "The Workmen's Circle and all the others? That's what I want to know!"

Workers crowded into the Labor Lyceum for their union meetings.

Rose stared at one person and then another. Sophie hadn't seen her so animated since the day she'd been arrested.

Shane held up his hand. "It's true we have had our disappointments. But we have had moral support from a number of Jewish organizations."

"You can't eat moral support," said Ethel.

"And—" Rose began to stand up, but then quickly sat down again.

"But you must understand," Shane continued. "Many forces beyond our control have been working against us. There's massive unemployment from coast to coast. And who knows when or how it will end?" He glanced at his notes and gazed at the sparse audience. "I can report that, so far, thirty-five dressmaking firms have agreed to the union's demands; twenty-one have not."

"So what are we going to do?" Sadie said.

"A good question," Rose murmured.

"Your executive advises you to continue to strike," Shane said.

There was a general murmur in the hall, a scraping of chairs, a clearing of throats. Everyone started to talk at the same time.

"I'm at the end of my rope!"

"So you'll make the rope a little longer!"

"Maybe the Communist union is better."

"Maybe yes. Maybe no."

"What are you talking about? We have to stick together!"

"Who knows how long it will last?"

"It'll last as long as it lasts."

The arguments went on and on. People started shouting and gesturing, and it looked as if several might come to blows. A few people walked out, shouting, "I've had enough!"

In the midst of this hubbub, Rose stood up and slowly made her way down the aisle to the podium. Sophie was about to stop her, but then she saw the determined look on Rose's face.

Shane made a slight bow, introduced Rose, and sat down heavily on a chair. He took a large white handkerchief out of his pocket and mopped his forehead.

Rose licked her lips and began to speak. "Fellow workers…" The feedback from the microphone made a screeching sound and people put their hands up to their ears. Shane adjusted the mike and quickly sat down again.

"Fellow workers, I won't tell you what I went through in jail." Rose shuddered. "Actually, I'm trying to forget the whole experience. But one thing I know for sure."

"What's that?" Sadie said.

"Let her talk already!" said Morris the Presser.

Rose spoke slowly and enunciated every word. "We must all stick together. Our only hope for success lies in unity. Otherwise, we will fail. And then we'll be back where we started—maybe even worse off—with long hours, terrible working conditions, and low pay."

"She's right," Herman the Cutter said. "We have to stay on strike."

Rose raised her hand. "And one more thing." She nodded in the direction of Bernard Shane. "We'll end up without a strong union to support us."

Rose made her way back to Sophie as people shook her hand and patted her on the back. "I didn't think I could talk in front of people ever again," she whispered.

Sophie hugged her. "I'm *so* proud of you!"

"And I'm proud of *you!*" Rose hugged her back. The hug released the tension Sophie had been feeling for weeks. Somehow, she now felt some hope for the future.

The arguments continued for a few more minutes, but in the end the workers voted to continue to strike.

✄

Jake had finished selling his papers and was walking home along Spadina when he saw a crowd of people coming out of the Lyceum. He decided to hang around for a while in case Sophie was with them.

When he saw her coming out, he took a step forward, but then hesitated. She had her arm linked with another young woman who had the same curly hair and hazel eyes.

"Sophie?"

Sophie looked startled and began to blush. She looked at the other woman and hesitated. "Rose, this is Jake…Malone. Jake, this is my sister, Rose."

Rose raised her eyebrows. "Jake? I don't think I know you."

"But…I told you about him," Sophie said.

Rose pulled on Sophie's arm. "Come on, Sophie. We have to go home."

"But I want to talk to Jake…"

Rose pulled harder. "Mama's waiting. Come *on*!"

Jake tried to follow them but Sophie shook her head. As they walked away, Rose said, "You should know better! You shouldn't be talking to that goy!"

"But he's nice," Sophie said. "He's my friend."

"You can't be friends with a non-Jew. You know it never works out."

"This isn't Russia!" Sophie stopped walking and turned to face her sister. "This is Canada! It's a free country."

"It's free maybe for *them*. Not for us."

"But—"

Rose crossed her arms. "No buts. Do you want me to tell Mama? Doesn't she have enough worries?"

"But—"

"Sophie, I said come home and I *mean* it!"

Sophie looked back at Jake. Rose tugged her arm again.

Jake watched as she turned her back on him and walked away.

He gritted his teeth. He was mad as heck but he didn't know what to do. Sick with longing and disappointment, he plodded home along the lonely street.

CHAPTER 14
Help Yourself

"I hate you!" Sophie yelled when they got home. Mama was lying on the couch. The sound of her snoring filled the front room.

Rose shrugged. "Sticks and stones…"

"Why did you drag me away like that?"

Rose poured a glass of water from the tap and turned around to face her sister. "You know why. He's not Jewish. It can't work out." She gulped the water. "It's like oil and water, they don't mix."

"It's not like I'm going to marry him!" Sophie stood facing Rose, her hands on her hips. "It's not fair!"

"Who said life was fair?" Rose thought about her time in jail but quickly brushed the memory aside. "Anyway, if you start to date him," she continued, "it's the first step." She put the glass on the counter and plopped down on a kitchen chair.

"You're making a mountain out of a molehill!" Sophie flung her arm out and knocked the glass to the floor. It shattered into a thousand pieces.

"Did something break?" Mama called from the front room. "And why are you arguing?"

Rose looked at Sophie and put her finger to her lips. "It's nothing."

"Nothing, Mama." Sophie got the broom and dustpan from the corner and started cleaning up the mess. But she seethed inside, like a kettle about to boil over.

Later in the evening, there was a knock on the door. Sophie was sitting on the couch and for the third time was reading Papa's book of stories by Sholem Aleichem.

"She's not home," Rose said.

Sophie heard Jake say, "Give her a message for me. Will you, please?"

She sprang up and hurried to the door. "Rose, go away. Stay out of my business."

Rose blocked the door. "Your business is my business."

"Please, Rose. Just leave us alone for a few minutes."

Rose shook her head. "I won't." She turned to Jake and whispered, "Please leave before my mother comes." She began to shut the door.

"Who's there?" Mama called from the kitchen.

"Nobody, Mama," said Sophie.

Mama limped to the door and pushed her aside. "Let me see who this nobody is."

Rose opened the door wider. "This is Jake Malone, Sophie's friend," Rose said.

"Malone?" Mama looked at Jake, then at Sophie, and back at Jake. "Young man, you must go now." In Yiddish, she added, "Now you're inviting a *goy* into the house? Tell him he should not come back."

"But Mama—"

"Enough already!" Mama wagged her finger. "As long as you live in my house, you will not go out with *goyim*!"

Rose pushed Sophie aside. "I'll tell him."

"Don't you dare!"

Rose looked at Sophie with a mixture of pity and anger. "It's a hard world out there. You don't know how hard. And you don't need to make it worse than it is."

Sophie gritted her teeth and turned to Jake. "I'm sorry but my mother won't let me see you. It would be better if you don't come here again."

"But—"

"I'm really sorry, Jake. Please go now."

Jake took one last look at Sophie, sighed, and turned away. She had the feeling she would never see him again.

After Jake had gone, Mama said, "You should know better than to get involved with a non-Jew! After what Papa and I suffered in Russia from them!"

"Mama, this isn't Russia!"

Mama sank down on the couch. "Right. This is the Garden of Eden."

Sophie stomped into the bathroom, locked the door, and sat on the toilet seat. Her stomach was churning and her head was pounding. She wondered what Jake was feeling. If it was anything like the way she felt, he was utterly miserable.

Maybe she could sneak out of the flat and see Jake secretly. No one would have to know, would they? Maybe she and Jake could date for a few years, get married, then…

No, it was impossible. In their small, crowded corner of the world, no one could keep a secret. Everyone knew everyone else's business. But the most important reason was that Rose and Mama needed her and she couldn't let them down. Right here, right now, her family was the most important thing.

Maybe someday, somewhere, people wouldn't be wrapped up in prejudice. Maybe they would be able to judge others for what they really were. But the time was not now, and the place was not here.

Sophie and Rose lived in a flat on the second floor
of a row house like this one in present-day Toronto.

CHAPTER 15
May Day

"Hurry up!" Sophie was waiting for Rose by the front door. "The parade will be over before we get there!"

"Hold your horses!" Rose hurried to the tiny hallway, grabbed her coat, and fastened her hat with a pin.

Sophie teased, "I bet you want to look nice for that good-looking Ben."

Rose shrugged. "Oh, him. He's just a kid." She smiled like a cat that had swallowed a canary.

"He's older than you!"

Rose pushed her sister gently out the door. "Yeah. But I'm smarter than him."

"Girls!" Mama called. "Be sure you dress warmly. It's not summer yet!"

Mama had decided to stay home. Although she got around pretty well now that the cast was off her ankle, she still couldn't stand for long periods of time. Besides, starting on Monday, she had a job working at the hospital, and she didn't want to strain herself. Besides, she was busy preparing a "nice Friday night dinner." (With Mama there were always a lot of "besides.")

The strike was over! Sophie could hardly believe it, but it was truly, completely over! The week before, the union had signed four more contracts with employers; a hundred more workers had gone back to work.

Although some workers still hadn't signed new contracts, as far as Sophie could see, the strike had fizzled out. The workers were ready to go back, contract or no contract. On Monday the rest of them would finally stop marching and return to work.

Had they won or lost? Sophie wasn't sure. Some people said they had won because they had shown the owners that they wouldn't give in. They had stayed on the picket line for ten long weeks. They had suffered cold and hunger, boredom and abuse. Dozens of workers had been arrested. Many of them had been harassed by those so-called private detectives. The workers had watched the police ignore this brutality and instead guard the strike-breakers. But the strikers had stood their ground.

In the end, they had gained only part of what they wanted, and the owners probably wouldn't honor the contracts anyway.

Maybe other workers would be more successful in the future, and this strike had prepared the road ahead. And that was something.

The best news of all was that, with Mama and Rose working, Sophie could go back to school in the fall. She longed to finish high school and then go on to university. Maybe, just maybe, she could follow her dream to become a teacher.

She wasn't the same person she had been at the end of February when the strike began. She wasn't a naive kid anymore, but someone who had taken responsibility for her actions. She had stood up for herself, and for others as well.

The weather was cool but sunny on that May Day, and Sophie was enjoying the sunshine. She was sick and tired of the awful winter they'd gone through, fed up with always feeling cold, with slogging through slushy puddles, with the biting wind blowing on her chapped face.

The union met at the Lyceum and then lined up for the parade. Each group marched along Spadina behind its banner: the Labor Zionists, the Workmen's Circle, youth groups, schools, sports groups, and so on. At the rear walked some older men, their coat pockets bulging with newspapers, their heads together in discussions, their hands waving in the air to emphasize the points they were making. As they marched, bands played "The Internationale," and regular marches like Sophie's favorite, the "Colonel Bogey March."

The parade stopped at Bellevue Square Park, near Kensington Market. The crowd milled around a portable stage that had been set up. There were songs and speeches, but the highlight of the day came when Emma Goldman walked onto the stage. Sophie had heard a lot of talk about Goldman, but this was the first time she'd ever seen her.

She was a short, sturdily built woman, with brown hair pulled back in a bun and round glasses resting on a smallish nose. She looked briefly at her notes and then gazed out at the audience. The crowd quieted down. Sophie could even hear birds singing and the muffled sounds of traffic on Spadina.

"My friends," Goldman said in a clear, ringing voice. "Many of you have just finished a long, drawn-out strike. In these hard times, you stood up for what you believed. You fought for shorter hours, for safer working conditions, and most of all, you fought for your union."

"Hooray for the ILGWU!" Ethel shouted.

"Hip hip hooray! Hip hip hooray! Hip hip hooray!" the crowd answered.

Goldman held up her hand. Some stray hairs had escaped from her bun and she brushed them aside. "Believe me," she continued, "my heart goes out to you who have suffered for a cause. I know what it feels like to work in a sweatshop for ten or twelve hours a day. I know what it means to stand up for your beliefs and to be punished as a consequence."

Morris the Presser, who was standing behind Sophie, whispered, "She was put in prison, you know."

Herman the Cutter said, "Yeah, I know. For two years."

Sophie glanced at Rose, and saw that her face was pale and drawn. "Quiet, please," she whispered to the two men.

"Sorry," they muttered.

Goldman continued. "You fought for all those things, but most of all, you fought for your dignity, so you could make a living wage." She sighed. "We *all* have the right to earn a living—men and women. We know full well that, in the factories, women are often treated like second-class workers. They earn only a fraction of the pay for the same job men do." She smiled wearily. "This may sound like a revolutionary idea—of which, you know, I have many—"

"You sure do!" Sadie shouted.

"Pipe down!" Morris yelled.

"But I say today, it is only fair that women receive equal pay for equal work. Only in that way can a woman become independent. Only in that way will she be able to support herself."

Labor activist Emma Goldman fought for the rights of women garment workers.

"I want to be independent like that!" Sophie whispered.

Rose nodded. "Me too!"

Goldman leaned toward the audience. "There is one more point I wish to make today. If a woman cannot support herself, she is often forced to resort to a life of crime. I tell you, the criminal justice system is broken."

Rose shivered. Sophie put her arm around her sister's shoulders.

"Year after year, prisons return to the world a shipwrecked crew of humanity, their hopes crushed. With nothing but hunger and inhumanity to greet them, these victims soon sink back into crime as the only possibility of existence."

Rose leaned over and whispered in Sophie's ear, "I saw a lot of women like that in jail."

"Do you want to talk about it?"

"Later. I'll tell you all about it later."

Goldman straightened her back and counted on her fingers. "Three things I abhor above all: ignorance, superstition, and bigotry. These I will fight to the bitter end."

The crowd cheered and clapped. Goldman smiled and waited until they had quieted down. "My friends, every daring attempt to make a great change in existing conditions has been labeled Utopian. But we must continue to fight for our beliefs, and for what is right! And together, we shall overcome!"

After her speech was over, there was a brief question-and-answer period. Sophie felt glued to the spot. She wanted to ask a question but felt overcome with shyness. Goldman left the stage, and Bernard Shane and other union organizers crowded around her.

Sophie took a big breath, and pulled Rose toward the front. "Come on, Rose. I want to talk to her."

"To Emma Goldman? Are you kidding?"

"Come on!"

"Not me. You go ahead." Rose smiled. "I want to talk to Ben. Meet me at United Bakers in half an hour?"

The memory of sitting with Jake at United Bakers flashed through Sophie's mind. "No, not there. Let's meet at Walerstein's."

Rose shrugged. "Okay. Sure."

Sophie made her way through the laughing, milling crowd. She edged closer to Goldman and gathered her courage. "Miss Goldman?"

Goldman turned toward her and gazed at her with clear, blue-gray eyes. "Yes, my dear?"

"My name is Sophie Abramson."

"Were you one of the strikers?"

Sophie swallowed hard. "To the very end."

Goldman held out her hand and shook Sophie's. "You were very brave to stand up to the owners." She smiled at Sophie and her serious face seemed transformed, as if a ray of sunshine had come out from behind a cloud. "The world will need young women like you to lead the fight against tyranny and oppression."

Sophie blushed. "Can I really do that? I mean, fight against all that evil?"

Goldman put her hand on Sophie's shoulder. "You can if you are determined to. And Sophie?"

"Yes?"

"One of the weapons you will need is an education." Goldman sighed. "I myself had to leave school early and could not go to high school." She shook her head. " You know, my father once told me, 'Girls do not have to learn much. All a Jewish daughter needs to know is how to prepare gefilte fish, cut noodles fine, and give the man plenty of children.'" She squared her shoulders. "What I know, I learned for myself.

"Go back to school, Sophie Abramson. Read and study. Then you will be ready to fight whatever battles lie ahead." She placed her hand on Sophie's shoulder. "Will you do that, my dear?"

"I will, Miss Goldman. I will!"

The girls sat at a small table at Walerstein's, an ice-cream soda in front of each of them. The store was crowded with other people who had come from the parade. They jostled for chairs around the tables or sat on stools at the counter, greeted each other, shared pamphlets they had picked up, and talked about Goldman's speech.

Sophie sipped the soda slowly and tried to make it last as long as possible. "You said you'd talk to me later." She raised her chin. "Well, later is now."

Rose sighed and reached for her sister's hand. She related what had happened to her at the Mercer. Sophie knew she wasn't telling her everything, but she let it go. For the first time, the very first time, Rose was treating her as an equal.

"But that's all water under the bridge now." Rose wiped the tears from her eyes. "This strike was only the beginning. And, little sister, we've got a lot more fight in us yet!"

"We tried to make a great change. Didn't we, Rose?"

"Of course we did! And we'll keep trying!"

"Even if we couldn't change everything?"

Rose put her hand on Sophie's. "Even if we couldn't change everything."

"Do you remember how we used to come here with Papa?"

Rose nodded. "He used to stir a heaping teaspoon of sugar into his tea, and then another."

Walerstein's Ice Cream Parlour on Spadina Avenue was a popular spot for meeting friends.

"Yeah. I think he still had the mud of the Old Country on his shoes," Sophie said.

"He'd look at us with a twinkle in his eye. And he'd say, 'My darling daughters, the Golden Land this is not.'"

Sophie smiled at her sister. "On the other hand…"

"On the other hand, it's not so bad."

AUTHOR'S NOTES

Trade unions organized many strikes in Canada, especially during the first part of the twentieth century. These strikes involved men and women who labored in the needle trades and in many other industries such as mining, forestry, and fishing.

The ILGWU dressmakers' strike in Toronto lasted from February 25 to May 1, 1931. Because of the worldwide slump in the economy during the Depression, the strike was ultimately unsuccessful in achieving the goals of the workers. However, union organizers learned valuable lessons from the strike and eventually achieved recognition of the union and better working conditions for the laborers.

Unfortunately, tens of thousands of workers in many parts of the world today—men, women, and even children—do not have the opportunity to join a union. Many work in unsafe and unhealthy conditions. They are often overworked and underpaid; when they are mistreated, they have no way to voice their complaints. If they are sick or injured, they receive little help. For many, a union is the only way the workers can gradually improve the quality of their lives and those of their families.

ABRAHAM CAHAN (1860–1951) was born in Belarus and immigrated to New York City in 1882. He was a socialist newspaper editor, novelist, and politician. He founded the *Jewish Daily Forward (Forverts)* in 1887 and ran the newspaper full-time until 1946. Cahan's writing in the *Jewish Daily Forward* and his commitment to socialism influenced many Jewish immigrants in the United States and beyond.

DAVID EDELSTADT (1866–1892) whose lines of poetry begin this book, was born in Russia, where he published his first poem at the age of twelve. In 1882, at the age of fifteen, he immigrated to the United States and settled in New York City. He was a buttonhole-maker by trade and wrote poems in Yiddish about the workers' struggle for dignity and freedom. Amid the terrible conditions in the sweatshops and tenements in New York, he contracted tuberculosis, from which he died at the age of twenty-six. Emma Goldman described Edelstadt as a man with "a fine idealistic nature…whose songs of revolt were beloved by every Yiddish-speaking radical."

EMMA GOLDMAN (1869–1940) was known for her political activism, writing, and speeches, especially regarding anarchist philosophy, women's rights, and social issues. Born in Lithuania, she immigrated to the United States in 1885—first to Rochester, New York, and then to New York City. In Rochester, Goldman worked as a seamstress, sewing overcoats for more than ten hours a day, earning two and a half dollars a week. During her life, Goldman was described as a free-thinking rebel by admirers, and denounced by critics as an advocate of politically motivated murder and violent revolution. After being deported from the United States for her anarchist (and illegal) activities, she lived in England, France, and Canada. She died in Toronto at the age of seventy.

BERNARD SHANE, the American manager of Local 1 of the ILGWU, conducted strikes in Toronto in 1929–1931 and was later sent to Canada in 1934 to organize the Toronto cloak-makers. Attempts at bringing the Toronto dressmakers into the union finally succeeded when 800 workers joined Local 72. At the end of the 1930s, the Toronto Joint Board obtained the first collective agreement for the dress industry when it signed fifty shops representing one thousand members.

Yiddish expressions in the text are taken from Shirley Kumove's *Words Like Arrows: A Collection of Yiddish Folk Sayings* (Toronto: University of Toronto Press, 1984).

When my father, Morris Dublin, came to Canada in 1948, he immediately got a job in a men's tailoring shop. He joined a strong union, worked in tolerable conditions, and earned a decent wage. He never went on strike. He was one of the lucky ones.

FURTHER READING

√ **Books for children or teens are indicated by a checkmark.**

A Common Thread: A History of Toronto's Garment Industry. Toronto: Beth Tzedec Congregation, 2003.

√ Auch, Mary Jane. *Ashes of Roses.* New York: Henry Holt, 2002.

Cotter, Charis. *Toronto Between the Wars: Life in the City, 1919-1939.* Richmond Hill, ON: Firefly, 2004.

√ Dash, Joan. *We Shall Not Be Moved: The Women's Factory Strike of 1909.* New York: Scholastic, 1996.

√ Ellis, Sarah. *Days of Toil and Tears: The Child Labour Diary of Flora Rutherford*. Richmond Hill, ON: Scholastic, 2008.

Friesner, Esther. *Threads and Flames*. New York: Viking, 2010.

Glazebrook, G.P. de T. *A Shopper's View of Canada's Past: Pages from Eaton's Catalogues, 1886–1930*. Toronto: University of Toronto Press, 1969.

√ Gourley, Catherine. *Good Girl Work: Factories, Sweatshops, and How Women Changed Their Role in the American Workforce*. Brookfield, CT: Millbrook, 1999.

√ Greene, Jacqueline Dembar. *The Triangle Shirtwaist Factory Fire*. New York: Bearport, 2007.

√ Greenwood, Barbara. *Factory Girl*. Toronto: Kids Can Press, 2007.

√ Haddix, Margaret Peterson. *Uprising*. New York: Simon & Schuster, 2007.

√ Hopkinson, Deborah. *Hear My Sorrow: The Diary of Angela Denoto, a Shirtwaist Worker*. New York: Scholastic, 2004.

Marrin, Albert. *Flesh and Blood So Cheap: The Triangle Fire and Its Legacy*. New York: Knopf, 2011.

√ Nodelman, Perry. *Not a Nickel to Spare: The Great Depression Diary of Sally Cohen*. Richmond Hill, ON: Scholastic, 2007.

√ Paterson, Katherine. *Bread and Roses, Too*. New York: Clarion Books, 2006.

√ Paterson, Katherine. *Lyddie*. New York: Lodestar, 1991.

Rudahl, Sharon. *A Dangerous Woman: The Graphic Biography of Emma Goldman*. New York: The New Press, 2007.

√ Sachs, Marilyn. *Call Me Ruth*. Garden City, NY: Doubleday, 1982.

Spiesman, Stephen A. *The Jews of Toronto: A History to 1937*. Toronto: McClelland and Stewart, 1979.

WEBSITES

Kelley, Mark. "Made in Bangladesh" on *The Fifth Estate*. CBC.ca, Oct. 4, 2013. http://www.cbc.ca/player/Shows/ Shows/the%20fifth%20estate/Web%20Exclusives/ ID/2410441647/.

Kelley, Mark. "After the Cameras Went Away: Made in Bangladesh" on *The Fifth Estate*. CBC.ca, April 23, 2014. http://www.cbc.ca/player/Shows/Shows/the+fifth+estate/ ID/2451379013/.

The Kheel Center ILGWU Collection: http://www.ilr.cornell.edu/ilgwu/.

ACKNOWLEDGMENTS

Archivists: Archives of Ontario, City of Toronto Archives, Multicultural History Society of Ontario (Cathy Leekam), Ontario Jewish Archives (Melissa Caza, Brooky Robins, George Wharton); Naomi Bell, for her continuing friendship as well as her expert translation of articles from the 1930s Toronto Yiddish newspaper, *Der Yiddishe Zhurnal*; Ruth A. Frager, Associate Professor, Dept. of History, McMaster University, Hamilton, Ontario, who asked some hard questions and gave me helpful comments on an early draft of the book; Sam Gindin, director of research for the Canadian Auto Workers (CAW) union 1974–2000, Visiting Packer Chair in Social Justice 2000–2010 in the Political Science Department at York University, Toronto; Bill Gladstone, publisher and columnist at the *Canadian Jewish*

News, for his perceptive editorial comments and breathtaking knowledge of Ontario Jewish history; Amanda Glasbeek, Associate Professor (Criminology), Department of Social Science, York University, Toronto, for insights and information about the Mercer Reformatory; Bernard (Mel) Katz, former Head, Archival and Special Collections, University of Guelph Library, Guelph, Ontario; Lynne Kositsky, for her reminiscences about her father's blouse factory in London, England; Ruthie Ladovsky, United Bakers Dairy Restaurant, Toronto, who always greets her customers with a smile; Dorion Liebgott, Curator, Beth Tzedec Reuben & Helene Dennis Museum, Beth Tzedec Synagogue, Toronto; Catherine Macleod, author of "Women in Production: The Toronto Dressmakers' Strike of 1931" in *Women at Work: Ontario, 1850–1930*, for steering me in the right direction when this book was just the glimmer of an idea; Ester Reiter, Associate Professor, Department of Social Sciences and the School of Women's Studies, York University, Toronto, who shared with me some of the viewpoints and activities of radical women in Canada during the 1920s and 1930s; My writing group, as ever: Rona Arato, Sydell Waxman, Lynn Westerhout, Frieda Wishinsky—for insightful comments, emotional support, and lots of laughs. Others who helped along the way: Beatrice Barzilai, Matilda Bigio, Fela Carmiol, Max and Julia Dublin, Morris Dublin z"l, Dorry Korn, Janna and Michael Nadler, Yitz Penciner z"l, Izzy Rabinovitch, Judy Saul, Sheryn Weber. For Second Story Press: Gena K. Gorrell, editor extraordinaire, and Carolyn Jackson, Melissa Kaita, Michelle Melski, and always, Margie Wolfe.

PHOTO CREDITS

page 4: public domain
page 9: Ontario Jewish Archives, item 3308.
page 14: public domain
page 26: Dressmakers General Strike, 1931. Ontario Jewish Archives, Item 1440.
page 28: City of Toronto Archives, Fonds 1266, Item 8245.
page 40: City of Toronto Archives, Fonds 16, Series 71, Item 4082.
page 47: City of Toronto Archives, Series 71, Item 15135.
page 56: Ontario Jewish Archives, item 3673.

page 62: Frank W. Micklethwaite / Library and Archives Canada / e003894555 page 69: City of Toronto Archives, Fonds 1244, Item 10077.
page 79: Ontario Jewish Archives, fonds 83, file 9, item 35.
page 105: City of Toronto Archives, Fonds 1266, Item 23262.
page 114: Anne Dublin
page 119: public domain
page 123: Ontario Jewish Archives, item 1922.
page 136: Errol Young

ABOUT THE AUTHOR

Anne Dublin is a former teacher-librarian and award-winning author living in Toronto. She has written two biographies: *June Callwood: A Life of Action* and *Bobbie Rosenfeld: The Olympian Who Could Do Everything*, as well as *Dynamic Women Dancers*, part of the Women's Hall of Fame Series. She has also written the children's historical fiction novel *The Orphan Rescue*. www.annedublin.ca